The Sociable Companions by Margaret Cavendish

Margaret Lucas Cavendish, Duchess of Newcastle-upon-Tyne was born in 1623 in Colchester, Essex into a family of comfortable means.

As the youngest of eight children she spent much time with her siblings. Margaret had no formal education but she did have access to scholarly libraries and tutors, although she later said the children paid little attention to the tutors, who were there 'rather for formality than benefit'.

From an early age Margaret was already assembling her thoughts for future works despite the then conditions of society that women did not partake in public authorship. For England it was also a time of Civil War. The Royalists were being pushed back and Parliamentary forces were in the ascendancy.

Despite these obvious dangers, when Queen Henrietta Maria was in Oxford, Margaret asked her mother for permission to become one of her Ladies-in-waiting. She was accepted and, in 1644, accompanied the Queen into exile in France. This took her away from her family for the first time.

Despite living at the Court of the young King Louis XIV, life for the young Margaret was not what she expected. She was far from her home and her confidence had been replaced by shyness and difficulties fitting in to the grandeur of her surroundings and the eminence of her company.

Margaret told her mother she wanted to leave the Court. Her mother was adamant that she should stay and not disgrace herself by leaving. She provided additional funds for her to make life easier. Margaret remained. It was now also that she met and married William Cavendish who, at the time, was the Marquis of Newcastle (and later Duke). He was also 30 years her senior and previously married with two children.

As Royalists, a return to life in England was not yet possible. They would remain in exile in Paris, Rotterdam and Antwerp until the restoration of the crown in 1660 although Margaret was able to return for attention to some estate matters.

Along with her husband's brother, Sir Charles Cavendish, she travelled to England after having been told that her husband's estate (taken from him due to his being a royalist) was to be sold and that she, as his wife, would receive some benefit of the sale. She received nothing. She left England to be with her husband again.

The couple were devoted to each other. Margaret wrote that he was the only man she was ever in love with, loving him not for title, wealth or power, but for merit, justice, gratitude, duty, and fidelity. She also relied upon him for support in her career. The marriage provided no children despite efforts made by her physician to overcome her inability to conceive.

Margaret's first book, 'Poems and Fancies', was published in 1653; it was a collection of poems, epistles and prose pieces which explores her philosophical, scientific and aesthetic ideas.

For a woman at this time writing and publishing were avenues they had great difficulty in pursuing. Added to this was Margaret's range of subjects. She wrote across a number of issues including gender, power, manners, scientific method, and philosophy.

She always claimed she had too much time on her hands and was therefore able to indulge her love of writing. As a playwright she produced many works although most are as closet dramas. (This is a play not intended to be performed onstage, but instead read by a solitary reader or perhaps out loud in a small group. For Margaret the rigours of exile, her gender and Cromwell's closing of the theatres mean this was her early vehicle of choice and, despite these handicaps, she became one of the most well-known playwrights in England)

Her utopian romance, 'The Blazing World', (1666) is one of the earliest examples of science fiction. Margaret also published extensively in natural philosophy and early modern science; at least a dozen books.

She was the first woman to attend a meeting at Royal Society of London in 1667 and she criticized and engaged with members and philosophers Thomas Hobbes, René Descartes, and Robert Boyle.

Margaret was always defended against any criticism by her husband and he also contributed to some of her works. She also gives him credit as her writing tutor.

Perhaps a little strangely she said her ambition despite her shyness, was to have everlasting fame. During her career, from the mid 1650's until her death, she was prolific. In recent decades her work has undergone a resurgence of interest propelled mainly by her ground-breaking attitude and accomplishments in those male straitened times.

Margaret Cavendish died on 15th December 1673 and was buried at Westminster Abbey.

Index of Contents

THE SOCIABLE COMPANIONS

THE CAST LIST
Master Save-all
Captain Valour
Lieutenant Fightwell
Cornet Defendant
Will Fullwit
Harry Sencible
Dick Traveller
Get-all, an Usurer
Serjeant Plead-all, a Lawyer
Doctor Cure-all, a Physitian
Roger and Tom, Get-all's two Men
Two other Men, one the Serjeants, the other the Doctors
A Drawer
Mistress Peg Valourosa, Sister to Captain Valour
Mistress Jane Fullwit, Will Fullwit's Sister
Mistress Anne Sencible, Harry Sencible's Sister
Mistress Informer, an old decay'd Gentlewoman
Mistress Prudence, Daughter to Master Save-all
Several Wooers, and Others

ACT I

SCENE I

[Enter **COLONEL**, **CAPTAIN**, **LIEUTENANT**.

COLONEL
What News, Captain?

CAPTAIN
It is an old saying, That ill News hath wings, and good News no legs.

COLONEL
Hath thy News wings, or no legs?

CAPTAIN
It hath wings; for it is reported for certain, that the Army shall be disbanded, and all the Soldiers Cashiered.

LIEUTENANT

So, then the Army will be a flying Army.

CAPTAIN

But yet we must beg upon Crutches.

LIEUTENANT

I believe we should have been stronger, if we had been of any other Profession, having had a better employment to have busied our minds and persons with; for Soldiers for the most part, their time and lives are idle, having no great employment or business, but when they march or fight, which is not every day or week; and when we are in Quarters or Trenches, we have nothing to do but to watch by turns; and therefore we are forced (for want of better employment) to pass our time with the Wenches in the Suburbs, or the Baggages that follow the Army, with whom we get the Pox.

CAPTAIN

But how shall our Pocky bodies live, if we be Cashier'd?

LIEUTENANT

We must endeavour to get into some Hospital for Cure.

COLONEL

That will be more difficult, then to get into a Court for Preferment, Lieutenant.

CAPTAIN

The truth is, we may more easily get into a Court, then to have a Cure in an Hospital; and we may more easily be cured in an Hospital, then get Preferment in a Court; for Soldiers are never regarded in time of peace; for when a War is ended, Soldiers are out of Credit.

COLONEL

And in time of War Courtiers are out of fashion.

CAPTAIN

Faith, Soldiers regard not new Modes, no more then Wars give ear to Flattery.

LIEUTENANT

But Courtiers do oftener turn Soldiers, then Soldiers Courtiers.

COLONEL

Faith, Lieutenant, much alike; for Courtiers are too weak to make Soldiers, and Soldiers are too rough to make Courtiers.

LIEUTENANT

How, come Courtiers weak, Colonel?

COLONEL

As Soldiers come weak; for Courtiers bring the Pox into an Army, and the Soldiers carry it out of an Army; for there is no resemblance between a Courtier and a Soldier, but by that disease; for the Pox make Courtiers and Soldiers like unto like.

CAPTAIN
Well, leaving the Pox to the Courtiers, how shall we that are Soldiers, live?

LIEUTENANT
We must rob on the King's high-way.

CAPTAIN
So we may chance to be hang'd.

LIEUTENANT
If we be, the care of a livelihood will be at an end.

CAPTAIN
But I would not venture my life for a little mony.

LIEUTENANT
How ignorantly you talk Captain! for do not all Soldiers venture their lives in Battel for other mens sakes or Quarrels, and have no reward for their venture and danger? and will such Soldiers be afraid to venture their lives for themselves, and their lives maintenances?

CAPTAIN
But there is hope to escape death in a Battel, but there is no hopes for a man to escape death when as his neck is in a nouse.

LIEUTENANT
There is as little hopes to escape death when as we have no means to live; and for my part, I had rather be hang'd then starv'd; but howsoever, I am a Soldier both in spirit and profession, who fears not death; and you seem to be a Soldier in name, and not in nature; you have the title of a valiant warring man, which is a Soldier, and the nature of a Coward; otherwise, you would not talk of escaping death, which shews you fear death.

CAPTAIN
If you were not my approved friend, you should find I were no Coward as to fear to fight with you; but I am afraid to die a base death, as a thief, and not like a Soldier.

COLONEL
How strangely you talk, Captain! are not all Soldiers thieves? Do not all Soldiers Plunder? Do not they take the Spoiles of their Enemies? As first, kill their enemies, or take them prisoners, and then seise on their goods, and all by Force? and all Force is Hostility, and Hostility Robbery; and do not only the common Soldiers, but we Commanders, nay, our Generals do the same? and yet you name Thievery and Robbery base, which baseness you and many more of all degrees and qualities have practised and lived with this dozen years to my knowledge, and it hath been a practise ever since the world began: for Adam and Eve robbed Gods Appletree, for they were forbid to take, or eat, and yet they did both; and did not Cain kill his brother Abel? and was not the Devil an enemy from the beginning? Thus Robbery,

Malice, Murder and Disobedience begun from the worlds Creation, and will last to the worlds Dissolution; by which we may see, that our profession, which is to rob, fight and kill, is the most ancient profession that is.

LIEUTENANT
Dear Colonel, you have spoken most learnedly and truly.

CAPTAIN
But yet there is difference between a Robber, a Murderer, and a Soldier; for it is Honourable to Kill our Enemies in the open Field: and it is Lawful to possess the Spoiles.

COLONEL
Many times we Kill our Friends, especially in Civil Warrs; and when we Fight with Foreigners, they never did us hurt, injury, or malice; but what do you talk of such Honour as Warring-Honour, which is a fair Name to a foul Act; and of such Martial Law, as is Lawless and most unjust, as to take away other Mens Rights? 'tis all one to call black white, or white black. But there is no such thing as Law, nor no such thing as Honour, but what Man feigns or makes; but the truth is, that which Men call Law and Honour, is Power and Force: for, the Strongest give Law; and Power makes Honour as it pleases.

CAPTAIN
Your learned discourse, Colonel, shall not perswade me to Rob on the High-way.

LIEUTENANT
What will you do then, Cap. to get a living?

CAPTAIN
I will think of some honester way to live.

COLONEL
You had best Trade, and cozen your Customers, that is a very honest way of Living; or serve and Cozen your Master, or deceive your Mistriss, that is an honest way of Living; or to Flatter some great Lord, or Lie with some Old Lady, that is an Honest way of Living: or betray, or accuse some Rich Man, to get a Morsel of his Estate for a Reward, that will be an honest Living: or Debauch a young Heir to live on his Luxuries and Riots, or Corrupt young Virgins and Married Wives with Pimping, that will be an honest and honourable Living: or be a Broker for the Courtiers, to help them to sell their old Clothes: or a Rook: or be a Huckster for the Courtiers, to bring them Suters and Petitioners for a share of their Bribes, that will be an honest Living: or frequent Taverns and Ordinaries that are customed with Noble Guests, and leave them to Pay thy Share, that will be an honourable Living; and an Hundred such waies there be, to get an honest Living.

CAPTAIN
No, I will go to Plow and Cart first.

LIEUTENANT
What? will you be a Slave to a Horses Tail?

COLONEL

No, no, I will tell you a better way for You, and the Lieutenant, and my Self to Live, than that: Let us get some of our Poor Whores that followed the Army; and go into some New-found Land, to help to increase Plantation.

CAPTAIN
Content Colonel, but let me tell you, it will be but a rotten Plantation.

COLONEL
Faith all Plantations are but rottenly begun; but the more rotten the Planters are, the better; for rottenness doth, like as dung, help to Manure the Land.

LIEUTENANT
Faith Colonel, I like your Proposition so well, as I would be there.

CAPTAIN
So do I, wherefore let us fit and provide for our Journey presently, and sing this Song.

[The SONG]
(I)
CAPTAIN
Let's go to our New Plantation;
Let's go to our New Plantation;
And there we do hope,
No fear of a Rope;
Nor hanging in that Blessed Nation.

(II)
LIEUTENANT
Let's go to our New Plantation;
Let's go to our New Plantation;
For here's no Regard,
Nor Soldiers Reward,
In this most Wicked Nation.

(III)
COLONEL
Let's go to our New Plantation;
Let's go to our New Plantation;
Each Man with his Whore,
Although We be poor,
And Rottenness is our Foundation.

[At the end of the Song, Enters **PEG VALOROUS**.

PEG
Then the Captain sings the burden of an old Ballet.

CAPTAIN

Get thy coat Peg,
Get thy coat Peg,
Get thy coat Peg,
Get thy coat Peg, and go away with me.

PEG
You seem to be very merry Brother, that your Officers and you sing so cheerfully.

LIEUTENANT
By your favour Mistress, some for Joy do weep, and some for Sorrow sing; witness the Lamentation, and the Poetical Swan; and Tears are often produced by Laughter.

PEG
What is the the cause of your sorrowful singing?

CAPTAIN
The Army is Cashiered; and so the Soldiers are undone.

PEG
It were better the Soldiers should be undone, than the Kingdom.

CORNET
Will you speak against your Brother's Profession?

PEG
Yes, if it be for the general Peace of my Native Country.

CAPTAIN
But now there is Peace, how shall we live?

PEG
You must live in Peace by your Wits, as you lived in the Wars by your Valours.

LIEUTENANT
But all the Cavalier Party lost their Wits when they lost their Estates.

PEG
Then you must Petition the State of this Kingdom to build so large a Bethlam as to put in all the poor mad Cavaliers.

CAPTAIN
Your advice is good, and you shall deliver their Petition, Peg; but before I go to Bethlem I will go tell Harry Sensible and Will Fullwit the News.

LIEUTENANT
And the Cornet and I will go drink some Cordial Waters to revive our Spirits.

[Enter **ANNE SENSIBLE**, and **JANE FULLWIT**.

ANNE
Do you hear the News of the Cashiered Army?

PEG
Yes.

JANE
And are not you troubled at the News?

PEG
No; for I had rather my Brother should be poor with Safety, then rich with Danger; but your Brothers, although they have not been such Active sufferers, yet they have been Passive sufferers.

JANE
Yes, faith, they have had their shares of Losses; but now my Brother is poor, he begins to study.

PEG
What doth he study, his Losses?

JANE
No, he studies Books.

PEG
What books? the Crumbs of Comfort, and the Soveraign Salve, for the Cure of the Soul?

JANE
All our Brothers had need to Study and read a Cure for their Estates; but let us go and bear them Company.

[Exeunt **ANNE** and **JANE**.

[Enter **MISTRESS PRUDENCE** to **PEG**.

PRUDENCE
Cousin Peg, where is your Companions, Nann and Jane?

PEG
They are in their Chamber, envying your good Fortune, and repining at their own ill Fortune.

PRUDENCE
What good Fortune do they envy me for?

PEG
For being the only Child, and so the only Heir to a rich Father.

PRUDENCE

If their Brothers had been as wise as my Father, not to have been so vain to have show'd their Valour, they might have been so prudent as to have kept their Estates; and so you and they would not have lost your Portions by the folly of your Brothers.

PEG
It was not through their Folly, but through their Loyalty that they entered into the action of War.

[Enter **NAN** and **JANE**.

NAN
O Mistress Prudence! 'tis a wonder to see you abroad, or at home without a Gallant.

PRUDENCE
When I come to see great Beauties, such as you are, I dare not bring any of my Gallants, for fear you should rob me of them.

JANE
It would be a Charity to bestow some of the richest of your Suiters among us poor Virgins, to make Husbands of; and to chuse one of the poorest of our Brothers to be your Husband.

PRUDENCE
Indeed it would be a Charity to your Brothers, but no Charity to my self.

[Enter **MASTER SAVE-ALL**, Mistress Prudence's Father.

SAVE-ALL
Save you young Beauties.

PEG
We know not whether our Beauties will save us; but we shall hardly save our Beauties long; for old Father Time will take them from us.

SAVE-ALL
Then you must get good and rich Husbands in the time of your Beauties.

PEG
There are three difficult things to get; as first, to get a Husband; next, a good Husband; and last, a rich Husband; for Men care not for handsome Wives, but rich Wives; for had not my Cousin Prudence, your Daughter, Wealth as well as Beauty, she might have many Lovers, but not a Husband amongst them all.

SAVE-ALL
Cousin Peg, you may get a rich Husband, not only by the means of your Beauty, but by your Wit.

PEG
I have heard, that in former Ages, that many Men did live by their Wits; but in this Age Wit is out of fashion, and so out of practise, and so poor, as 'tis almost strange

[Enter **CAPTAIN**.

SAVE-ALL
I am talking to your Sister my Cousin Peg, and I perceive she despairs of getting a Rich Husband.

CAPTAIN
She hath reason, being poor her self; wherefore Peg, and her two dear Friends, Mistress Anne, and Mistress Jane, must lead Apes in Hell.

ANNE
If the Devil hath as many Apes as Mens follies, we shall never be able to lead them all.

SAVE-ALL
For fear my Daughter should lead Apes in Hell, I will go and get her a Husband.

ACT II

SCENE I

[Enter **WILLIAM FULLWIT**, and set at a Table with many Books about him. He reads. Enter to **WILLIAM FULLWIT**, **CAPTAIN** and **HARRY SENSIBLE**.

HARRY
Baccus and Mercury help thee, and have mercy on thee, for I perceive you are falling into Perdition, as from a Drunkard to a Student; from a merry Companion, to a dull Stoick; from a Wit to a Fool.

WILL
I pray thee Harry leave me, for I am studying to be a wise Man.

CAPTAIN
Faith Will, Wisdom is not learned by the Book, but by Practise, which gets Experience; for Wisdom lives with living Men, more then with dead Authors: But prithee tell us, what Books are you reading?

WILL
I am reading Plutarch's Lives, Thucidides, Machiavel, Commineus, Lucan, Cæsars Commentaries, and the like.

HARRY
Why such Books, since you are neither Greek nor Roman? So that those Histories, or Historians of other Nations will not benefit thee, nor thy Native Country for their Laws, Customs, or Humours; for what are the Laws, Customs, Humours and Governments of the Romans, Greeks, Turks, or Persians to thee, or thy Native Country?

CAPTAIN
You say true, Harry; and what are their Wars, or Peace to us, unless the same Cause, the same Places, and the same Men, were again in our time? For put the case you were a General, and were to fight a Battel, and would make Cæsar your Pattern, it were a thousand to one but you would shew your self

rather a Fool, then a Cæsar; for first, the Causes of War would be different; the Scituation of War different; the Humours of the Soldiers different; the Habilements, Postures, and Breeding of the Men different; the Means, Supplies, Supports, Armes, Time, Place, and Seasons different: So that if later Commanders should follow the Precepts of former Commanders and old Warriers, they would be losers; and instead of being fam'd good Soldiers, get the reproach of being ill Conductors.

HARRY
You say right, Captain; and as for Foreign Government, History is of no use, unless you would bring an Innovation; for which, had you power to make Combustions, you would sooner ruine the Kingdom, then alter the Government; besides, in all Alterations, Fortune hath greater power, and is more predominant then Prudence: wherefore leave thy impertinent Studies.

WILL
I will take your Counsel.

[Enter **LIEUTENANT DRUNK**, and comes Reeling in.

LIEUTENANT
Captain—Captain—I would fain speak, very—fain speak a speech—but I shall be out of my speech, before I begin, and that would be a very fowl disgrace—to a man of parts.

CAPTAIN
'Tis true, Lieutenant; but a drunken man hath no parts, for he is a departed man, Lieutenant.

LIEUTENANT
But I would have declared the strange effects—the Magical effects—the Mystical effects—and the Tyranical effects.

CAPTAIN
All which Effects meet in one Effect, which is to be drunk, Lieutenant.

LIEUTENANT
That is true Captain—but the strange Postures, several Humours, senceless Brains, and disabled limbs— is that which I would declare.

WILL
They will declare themselves, Lieutenant, without the help of Rhetorick.

LIEUTENANT
You are a fool, Will; for they will want help, as you may perceive by me—up—

[He Reels as he speaks.

WILL
But Words are too weak to support them.

LIEUTENANT
But Words may excuse them.

[Enter **MISTRESS PEG**.

PEG
Brother, there is a Gentlewoman without, that came with the Lieutenant, who says she will not go without him.

CAPTAIN
Lieutenant, there is a Gentlewoman stayes to support thee to thy rest.

LIEUTENANT
It is a Cousin of mine—newly come out of the Country—but I will go to her—up—

CAPTAIN
We will help to lead thee to her.

[They lead him forth.

[Exeunt **MEN**.

[Enter **MISTRESS JANE**, and **MISTRESS ANNE**, to **MISTRESS PEG**.

JANE
Where is the Lieutenant? 'tis said, he is so drunk, he can neither stand nor speak.

PEG
The truth is, he doth both, but ill-favouredly.

[Enter **MISTRESS INFORMER**.

PEG
Mistress Informer, you are welcome.

INFORMER
I know that, otherwise I would not visit you; but I seldom fail seeing you once a day, unless I be out of Town; but now I came out of Charity, knowing you were all alone.

PEG
How did you know we were all alone?

INFORMER
Because I met your Brother, Captain Valour, and Harry Sencible, Mistress Ann 's Brother, going up the Street.

JANE
Was not my Brother with them?

INFORMER

No; I saw Will Fullwit go to the Play-house.

JANE
What Play-house? the Gaming-house, or the Acting-house?

INFORMER
The Acting-house.

ANNE
Our Brothers might be so kind, as sometimes to carry us to Plays.

PEG
So they would, if we were such Cousins as the Lieutenant had here; but being their Sisters, they will not be troubled with us.

INFORMER
Now you talk of the Lieutenant, it puts me in mind, I met him in the Street leading a Gentlewoman.

PEG
I believe she rather led him, then he her.

INFORMER
I know not which, led which; but neither of them did walk steddily, for sometimes they went towads the Wall, and then presently towards the Kennel.

PEG
It was a sign they were both drunk. But Mistris Informer, have you brought the new-fashioned Hankerchief to see.

INFORMER
Yes, but I have left it in your Chamber.

PEG
Come let us go see it.

[Exeunt all but **JANE**.

[Enter **WILL FULLWIT** musted in his Cloak.

WILL
Sister Jane, is Harry Sencible within?

JANE
I cannot tell whether he be returned; but he was abroad?

WILL
Pray see; and if he be return'd, bid him come to me.

[Enter **HARRY SENCIBLE**, **WILL FULLWIT** upon the Ground, he groans, **HARRY SENCIBLE** runs and embraces him.

HARRY
Dear Will, what is the cause you lie so sadly?

WILL
Oh, oh, I am wounded, wounded.

HARRY
Where? where? tell me dear Will.

WILL
I am kill'd, I am kill'd.

HARRY
By whom?

WILL
I die, I die.

HARRY
Hold Life a little time, so long to tell thine Enemy, that I may sacrifice him on thy Tomb; Oh he is dead: dear Will, I wish to die, since thou art gone.

[Exit **HARRY SENCIBLE** Weeping.

[After he was gone out, **WILL FULLWIT** rises and Dances,— then enter **HARRY SENCIBLE**, with **CAPTAIN VALOUR**, **LIEUTENANT FIGHTWELL**, and **CORNET DEFENDANT**, all stand as in a Maze.

CAPTAIN
Harry, did not you tell us, that Will Fullwit was kill'd?

HARRY
I thought him dead.

CAPTAIN
Then how the Devil comes he to be alive again!

[Enter **MISTRESS ANNE SENCIBLE** as in hast.

ANNE
O, where is Mr. Fullwit 's body?

[He Addresses to her.

WILL
Dear Lady, I, for thy dear sake,

Will travel to the Stigean Lake;
There let us meet, and then imbrace,
And look each other in the Face.

ANNE
O the Lord, what doth he ayle?

[Enter **MISTRESS PEG VALOUROSA**.

WILL
O stand away,
For there breaks day;
The Sun doth rise,
Dazling mine Eyes:
For you the Goddess are of Light,
She's a fiend that governs Night.

HARRY
By heaven he is stark mad.

[**WILL FULLWIT** draws his Sword.

WILL
Here will I fight
As Champion Knight.

[The **LADIES** run squeeling away.

WILL
What, are they gon?
They do me wrong.

LIEUTENANT
You have frighted them away.

HARRY
Dear Will, put up thy Sword, for we are all thy Friends.

WILL
You are my Foes, I say,
Wherefore away.

HARRY
This madness is worse, far worse then death.

[**HARRY SENCIBLE**, Weeps.

WILL

What Harry, do you weep in earnest?

HARRY
How can I chuse, to see my friend in a mad distemper?

WILL
Why Harry, I have only acted an Intrigue.

CAPTAIN
A pox of your Intrigue; for you have frighted the Ladies, and disturbed your Friends.

LIEUTENANT
Nay faith, he hath disturbed the Ladies, and frighted his Friends.

HARRY
But how came you to be in this humour?

WILL
With seeing a new Play.

CORNET
But you have not acted an Intrigue yet.

WILL
That's true, by reason the Ladies went away, and Harry 's Tears would not suffer me to make more changes; besides I had not time to express, or act my Intrigue; but if you will call the Ladies again, you shall see me act an Intrigue and Catastrophe, as it ought to be.

HARRY
Hang Intrigues and Catastrophes, and play the fool no more.

CAPTAIN
Prithee Will, go with us to a Tavern, and there we will have several sorts of Wine, changes of Musick, and variety of Mistresses, which are better Intrigues and Catastrophes then are acted upon the Stage.

WILL
Content, let us go, to dry up Harry's Rhume with Sack, and to let him see I am still a merry Companion.

HARRY
If I had known you had dissembled, I would not have discovered my love.

WILL
Why? Love and Deceit is an Intrigue; but the truth is, I did this, that you and the Captain should not believe that I was a dull Stoick.

[Enter **DICK TRAVELLER**, as newly return'd home.

WILL

Dick Traveller, art thou return'd, old blade, from thy Foreign Travels, to thy home-Friends?

DICK
I confess Foreign Travellers are apt to lose home-Friends.

WILL
But you have not lost us, for thou art heartily welcome.

HARRY
'Tis a sign that your Travels have been as cold as far, for you have brought white Hairs home with you.

LIEUTENANT
He could not avoid a white head; for he hath been at the North Pole, which hath turn'd his Hairs to Snow.

DICK
I have been near the Pole in Greenland.

CORNET
Is that Country fertile?

DICK
Yes, of Frost and Snow.

CORNET
Is it Populous?

DICK
'Tis very populous of Bears and Foxes.

LIEUTENANT
Is it a good place for Plantation?

DICK
Yes faith, for if there were a Colony of Adulterers sent thither, they might Plant Chastity; and if a Colony of Drunkards were sent thither, they might Plant Temperance; also if a Colony of Prodigals were sent thither, they might Plant Frugality.

WILL
But might not a Colony of Fools plant Wit there?

LIEUTENANT
It were excellent Policy, to send all the Fools thither.

DICK
Those Parts of the World would not hold them, if all be sent; for most Men are Fools.

CAPTAIN

Why fools in what part of the World soever, they live in Twilight; and neer the Pole is Twilight half the year.

WILL
Prithee let's leave talking of such cold Elements; for the very hearing of the North Pole hath chil'd my Spirits, as if they were hard frozen, and all my thoughts are turn'd to Snow; wherefore let's go to a Tavern, and drink Sack to thaw them.

DICK
I shall bear you Company.

WILL
Faith thou hast reason to drink ten Fathom deep to melt thy frozen body, and thaw thy cold blood that is turn'd to Ice, that Spirits of life may swim in full large Veines.

DICK
You are full of Poetical fancy.

WILL
'Tis a sign I did never travel to the North Pole, for fancy lies in East and Western brains; the truth is, every Poets brain is a Torrid Zone; wherefore let's go to the Tavern.

HARRY
That is under the Ecliptick Line.

[Enter **PEG** and **ANNE**.

CAPTAIN
Are you come to see the Intrigue?

PEG
No, but we are come to see, whether Will Fullwit be not dead again.

WILL
No; but I am not so well, but that these good fellows, are going to give me a Cordial.

DICK
To me these Ladies are Cordials.

WILL
You have not tasted them yet.

DICK
May I presume to salute you, Ladies?

[He Salutes them.

HARRY

How do you like them?

DICK
It is not a question to be asked, not I to give an answer.

CAPTAIN
Prithee come away, and leave Complementing.

[Exeunt **MEN**.

[Enter **JANE**.

PEG
Did you see Dick Traveller.

JANE
Yes, I met him, and all the crew of them.

PEG
I have seen thy Brother stark mad.

JANE
I never knew him otherwise.

ANNE
He did only shew an Intrigue.

[Enter **MISTRESS INFORMER**.

PEG
Mistress Informer, you are welcome; but what News brought you hither?

INFORMER
Hearing Master Traveller was to see you.

PEG
He was so.

INFORMER
Pray what new fashions hath he brought from the North Pole?

PEG
I do not perceive any new fashion.

INFORMER
Lord, how reports prove false! for I heard he had a strange fashioned Suit of Clothes which he did wear, made all of Ice, and a great thick Cap of Snow, which he wore over his head; and that the motions of his Body and Behaviour were trembling and shaking, as if he were affrighted, or in a cold fit of an Ague, and

that his language was such a stuttering and stammering language, as not any man in these parts could understand him.

PEG
I saw no such Clothes or Cap that he wore, nor heard no such stuttering, stammering language.

INFORMER
Indeed, as to his Garments, I did not believe reports; for I said to those persons, that told that report for a certain truth, that I could sooner believe he was accoutred in a Suit of Fire, rather then of Ice; but they replyed, That those parts of the World, so neer the Poles, would not permit Fire; for the extream cold did put out all sorts of Fire; but pray tell me whether he doth not look very pale, wither'd, dry and old.

PEG
He doth not look as if he were a very young man, because he is in some years; but he looks well for his age.

INFORMER
What kind of Men, doth Mr. Traveller say, are the Natives at the Pole?

PEG
I did not hear him say, there be either native Men or Women.

INFORMER
If not, how did he get a Mistress?

JANE
Such colds Elements do not require Courtship.

INFORMER
But are there not any living Creatures there?

PEG
Yes, there are Bears; and in some of the Islands near the Poles, there are white Bears, with red Patches on their heads.

INFORMER
That is very fine, and surely very becoming; wherefore I will inform the Ladies, who I am sure will follow that fashion.

ANNE
How can they be in the Bears fashion?

INFORMER
Very easily; for they may have a white Sattin Gown, and a red Velvet Cap; and so be like the white Beares, with the red Patches on their heads.

PEG
If they imitate nothing else of the Bear but that, it will not be much a miss.

INFORMER
Fare you well; for I long to carry the News of the Fashion.

[Exit.

[Enter **WILL FULLWIT**.

WILL
Is Harry returned?

ANNE
No.

[Exeunt **WOMEN**.

[Enter **HARRY**.

WILL
I was going to the Tavern, believing you and the rest of our Companions, were gone to the Tavern.

HARRY
I stay for Dick Traveller; but Captain Valour, Lieutenant Fightwell, and Cornet Defendant, are gone before to the Tavern, to provide us good Wine.

WILL
They will be drunk before we come.

HARRY
Surely they will forbear drinking until we come.

WILL
How should they forbear drinking, if they went to tast the Wine?

HARRY
They went to bespeak good Wine, and not to tast it.

WILL
Hang them, they will tast pint after pint, and quart after quart; for they have not so much Temperance as to stay.

[Enter **DICK TRAVELLER**.

WILL
Dick, a Pox take you for staying, for the Captain, Lieutenant, and Cornet have drank all the Wine in the Tavern by this time.

DICK

They cannot drink all.

WILL
Yes but they can; for they will pour in and out so fast, as I am confident they have not left so much as the droppings of the Tapes.

HARRY
Come, come, let us make hast to them.

WILL
Yes, when all is drunk up.

HARRY
I will warrant you there will be enough left to quench our drought.

WILL
I hate quenching of droughts; I would be like a Ship, to swim in an Ocean of Wine.

[Enter **MISTRESS INFORMER**.

INFORMER
Are your Sisters within?

WILL
Yes.

[Exeunt **MEN**.

[Enter **PEG**, **JANE** and **ANNE**.

PEG
Mrs. Informer, what is the reason you are returned so soon?

INFORMER
The reason is, that I had forgot to tell you of the good company I was in the other day.

JANE
We heard that you were in Sociable Company.

INFORMER
I was so; and the Company hath past their time with all the delightful Recreations that could be devised, for the time they associated together; for sometimes the Ladies, and their courting Servants, play'd at Cards, and sometimes danced, and sometimes feasted, and some of the fairest Ladies sat to have their Pictures drawn, whilst their Lovers or Friends gazed on their Faces; which was an occasion to cause those Ladies to put their Faces into their best Countenances; and some of the Gallants did make their Mistresses Portraictures, both in Verse and Prose, whilst the Painter did draw their Pictures in Oyle or water-Colours.

PEG
It seems the Gallants were Courtly to the Ladies,

INFORMER
They were so.

JANE
Doth the Men court the Women publickly or incognito?

INFORMER
They Court both ways; for every Man hath, his particular, which he doth usher; but if they like each other's Lady and Mistress better then their own, or Love's variety, or would be liked, or loved by more then his own Woman: They make Love incognito, as in a Mistical or Allegorical way; which Allegorical-Love's making, or woings, pleases the women infinitely, as by eye-glances, languishing looks, smothered sights, and metaphorical speeches; as also wrying their Necks, with their eyes fixt on the ground, or falling, or stumbling upon them, as if it were by chance; and many the like Behaviours, Garbs, Motions, Countenances and Discourses, as I cannot remember to repeat all; and some are so excellent and well experienced in the Art of making Love incognito Allegorically, or Metaphorically, as I have known or observed one Man to make half a dozen Women at least at one time, believe he hath been deeply in Love with each of them.

JANE
And do the Women receive these fashioned Courtships in the like manner?

INFORMER
Yes, for they are as expert as the Men in those ways; the truth is, that although every Man and every Woman hath a Staple Servant, and a Staple Mistress, yet they traffick all in common.

JANE
It seems they are common Wooers: But farwell, I must go speak with my Brother Fullwit.

INFORMER
You must go to the Tavern then.

JANE
Why, is he gone to the Tavern?

INFORMER
Yes, I did hear him, Mr. Sencible, and Mr. Traveller say, they would go unto the Crown-Tavern.

PEG
I am sure my Brother and his Officer are there before them.

JANE
It is not to be endured they should spend so much, and we want so much as we do.

INFORMER
If I might advise you Ladies, I would have you go and bear them Company.

JANE

We will take your advice, although not to drink, yet to quarrel, and you shall be our Conductor.

PEG

Those that see us will believe that Mrs. Informer is a Bawd, that conducts three young Wenches to some Gentlemen in the Tavern.

INFORMER

Come, come, for if I be, it is not the first time I have been taken for a Bawd.

[Exeunt.

SCENE II

[Enter **CAPTAIN VALOUR, LIEUTENANT FIGHTWELL**, and **CORNET DEFENDANT**, as in a Tavern, who drink whilst they talk.

CORNET

Captain, let us not stay for Will, Harry and Dick, but drink in the mean time.

CAPTAIN

Content, let us sit close, and drink hard; for here is the best Wine; it was drawn out of Bacchus Cellar, wherefore it is divine Wine.

LIEUTENANT

If it be divine, we should pray before we drink.

CAPTAIN

No you must drink first, as into a drunken humour with divine Wine, and then pray when the Spirit is strong in you.

LIEUTENANT

It is unnatural, Captain, at least unusual for Martial men to pray; in so much, that if a Soldier should be seen or heard to pray, he would be thought a Coward.

CAPTAIN

That is not so, for we were beaten by those that Prayed.

CORNET

But some of our Party prayed.

CAPTAIN

If they did, it was so softly, as Jupiter could not hear them: But I have drunk my self into a loving humour, I wish I had a Wench.

CORNET
We will knock for the Chamberlain.

[Enter **CHAMBERLAIN**.

CAPTAIN
Chamberlain, get us some Wenches.

CHAMBERLAIN
There are none to be had, Sir.

CAPTAIN
You are a lying Rogue; for there hath been no age, nor there is not a Kingdom that is not fully stored with them.

CHAMBERLAIN
There is store in the Kingdom, if it please your Worship, but they are not for Soldiers in this age.

CAPTAIN
You lie, you Rogue, they are for Soldiers in all ages, even in the worst of times; for they will venture their lives to follow the Army for the pleasure of a Soldier.

CHAMBERLAIN
An't please your Worship, it is for the hopes of gaining some of the Soldier's Plunder; but now that your Worships can neither get Plunder nor Pay, they defie you, and will not come near you, but laugh at you, and say you are like old rusty Armes out of fashion, and that they are now for the Court, not for the Camp.

CAPTAIN
Dam'd Fortune, shall the Court rob us, both of wealth and pleasure?

[Enter **WILL FULLWIT**, **HARRY SENCIBLE**, and **DICK TRAVELLER**, the **CAPTAIN** drinking when they came in.

WILL
Hold, hold, Captain, what a Devil, are you mad to drink before we come?

CAPTAIN
You are mad to stay so long, would you have us choakt for thirst?

DICK
Come, come, we shall overtake them.

CAPTAIN
But you shall not, for we will, now you are come, sit and drink healths, as health for health.

WILL
Is there Wine enough to drink Healths?

CAPTAIN
Enough, Will, enough.

[They sit down and call for Wine.

CAPTAIN
Dick, you are not returned as a Traveller a la mode.

DICK
Would you have me a la mode de Bear, or a la mode de Fox.

CAPTAIN
Why not as well as other Travellers, that return a la mode de Ape, and a la mode de Ass?

WILL
Well, leaving the Bears, Foxes, Asses and Apes; here is a health to the North Star.

HARRY
That is a very cold Star, Will.

WILL
Therefore I will drink the health in Sack, to heat it into a Sun.

HARRY
And I will drink a health to Virtue.

CAPTAIN
You had better put Ice into your Wine then Virtue; for she is so cold, not any heat can thaw her; but I will drink a health more proper, for Dick Traveller's company, which are the seven deadly sins.

DICK
They belong more to the Courtier then the Traveller; yet I will pledge them, were they seventy seven sins, and drink them all at a draught.

LIEUTENANT
But that is unconscionabe to drink them all, leaving not any for your Friends.

DICK
All those I account my Friends, that have wit enough to get, or invent more; for new-fashioned Sins are as easily devised as new-fashioned Garments.

WILL
Who is the maker of new-fashioned Sins?

DICK
The Devil.

[Enter **JANE**, **ANNE**, **PEG**, and **INFORMER**.

CAPTAIN
But what the Devil makes these Women come hither?

WILL
Ladies, this is boldly done, to come and drink healths with us.

CAPTAIN
'Tis but changing of Sisters, and they will serve us for Wenches, and Mrs. Informer, my Cornet or Lieutenant shall pay her for their Company.

JANE
We came not to drink, but to complain that our Brothers should be so unkind, unworthy and unnatural, to sit drinking to fill their Heads, and empty their Purses, when we want Meat and Clothes.

PEG
You can be Jovial, but we must be Melancholy; you sing Catches, when we shed Tears.

ANNE
You have many Bottles of Wine, when we want Smocks to our backs.

WILL
But you have silk Gowns.

JANE
Yes, such as you buy at the second hand, or at some Broker's shop, which are more rotten then the Jews Clothes in the Wilderness.

HARRY
Why, what would you have us to do?

ANNE
Not to sit drinking in a Tavern most of your time; but to seek and endeavour to get some good Offices and Employments that may help to repair your ruins, and to maintain us according to our births and breedings.

WILL
Faith, we may seek, and not find; beg, and not get.

PEG
But yet you shall not need to spend that little which is left, in drink.

LIEUTENANT
If it were not for drink, we should run mad; but drink drowns all sorts of sorrows.

CAPTAIN
Leave your Caterwouling, and get you hence.

PEG
We will not go home, unless you will go with us.

WILL
Yes, so it will be thought, you are our Wenches, not known you are our Sisters.

JANE
We care not what people think, knowing our selves honest.

HARRY
Come, let us go, otherwise they will scould so loud, as all the Street will be in a hubbub to know the cause.

[Exeunt.

SCENE III

[Enter **FATHER** and his **DAUGHTER**.

FATHER
Daughter, you being now Marriageable, I am resolved to provide you a good Husband.

DAUGHTER
I am willing to be a Wife; but pray pardon me if I ask you what you mean by a good Husband?

FATHER
A good Husband, is a prudent Husband.

DAUGHTER
That is a miserable and jealous Husband.

FATHER
No, no, mistake me not, for miserableness and jealousie are extreams, but Prudence is a mean.

DAUGHTER
If I must marry according to a Moral mean, which is between extreams, then I must Marry a man of a mean Birth, mean Breeding, mean Estate, mean Wit, mean Judgment, mean Understanding, mean Esteem, mean Behaviour, and the like.

FATHER
No Daughter, I only desire you not to be an extream fool, as to marry to extream misery; but since you dispute for wisdom or discretion, I'le give you leave to make your own choice, which will tend either to my grief or comfort; to your own happiness or unhappiness; and I shall see whether you can act as wisely, as you plead wittily.

[Exit **SAVE-ALL**, and then enters a **SUITER**.

[Enter the **YOUNG LADY**.

SUITER
Madam, your Beauty is the Gaze or Blaze to all the World; nay, 'tis not only a mortal but an immortal Light, and as the soul, not of one humane Creature but of all the World; which immortal light and soul I am very desirous to enjoy, and to make you my Wife.

LADY
Sir, I shall readily consent, upon condition you make me a present of the Alkahest, and a jointure of the Elixir.

[Exit **LADY**, **SUITER** Solus.

SUITER
This Lady is not to be won with Complements of Learning.

[Enter another **GENTLEMAN**.

GENTLEMAN
Well met Sir; have you seen the Lady?

SUITER
Yes.

GENTLEMAN
And how do you agree?

SUITER
Just as Chymists and Fire.

GENTLEMAN
How is that?

SUITER
That is, they do not agree at all, but delude and cross each other.

GENTLEMAN
Nay, faith, if she be in a cross humour, I will not plead and present my suit to her to day.

SCENE IV

[Enter **HARRY**, and walks in a Musing Posture. Enter **CAPTAIN**.

CAPTAIN

What is the cause you walk in such a musing posture Harry?

HARRY
I have lost my Mistress.

CAPTAIN
Is that all?

HARRY
Yes, and too much.

CAPTAIN
Art thou mad?

HARRY
No.

CAPTAIN
Have you any Wit?

HARRY
Why do you ask?

CAPTAIN
Because you are Melancholy for a Woman.

HARRY
It would make you or any man Melancholy, to lose such a Woman as my Mistress is.

CAPTAIN
Faith, not unless my Mistress were the only Woman in the World.

HARRY
She was the only Woman in my affection.

CAPTAIN
'Tis a sign thy affection is a poor, mean, low, narrow, and little affection, that hath but one Room for one Mistress; whereas, my affection is as large as the Grand Signior's Seraglio,—for it will hold Hundreds of Mistresses, with all their Maids and Slaves attending upon them; the truth is, my affection will hold all the Women in the World; for I love all Women-kind, in so much as I can never want love so long as there be Women, or a Woman; and surely I can never want a Woman so long as the World doth last; for the World doth not increase any thing so numerously as Women; for all Armies, Nations, Cities, Towns, Villages, Houses, Churches and Chambers are for the most part filled with Women; and since there are so many Women, it were a madness for to be Melancholy for the loss of one woman: wherefore put off this whining humour for shame, and get another Mistress; and if I might advise you, I would have four and twenty Mistresses, at least, at one time, and so you will have a Mistress for every hour of the day and night.

HARRY
But my Mistress is a woman that doth excell all her Sex.

CAPTAIN
In what?

HARRY
In Beauty, Wit and Virtue.

CAPTAIN
Nay, if you talk of Virtue in a Mistress, you are mad indeed.

HARRY
May not a Man have a virtuous Mistress?

CAPTAIN
No, for it is against the rules and nature of virtue, to live in a Mistress; for virtue is an humble Servant, when as a Mistress is an imperious Tyrant; for Women are insolent and imperious so long as they are made Mistresses, which is to be flatter'd, attended and served with Mens estates, bodies and souls; but when they come to be wives, which is to be slaves, perchance, they may have so much of Virtue, as to be somewhat humble, when as they are forced to serve, and cannot command; but a wise Man will never have a Mistress, although he should live unmarried, but he will keep a Maid-servant for his use, and so take and turn away so often as he pleases: But is thy Mistress dead?

HARRY
No, but she is Married.

CAPTAIN
Why then, she may be her Husband's servant, and thy Mistress still?

HARRY
But she is too Virtuous to be my Mistress now she is another Man's Wife.

CAPTAIN
I prithee be not so wedded to the opinion of Womens Virtues; for that will hinder thee from pursuing a Lover's design.

HARRY
I will endeavour to forget this Mistress, and get another.

CAPTAIN
Now you speak like a wise Man.

[Enter **WILL** to the **CAPTAIN** and **HARRY**.

WILL
Captain, and Harry, I was even now wishing for either of you.

HARRY

If you be as fortunate in all your wishes, as in either of our being here, you will be the most fortunate and happiest Man that ever was; but tell us whether it it was your affection, appetite or reason, which was the cause of your wish.

WILL

Not any of them; for it was my wit that caus'dthat wish; for I have made a Copy of Verses, which I would have you both read, and then give me your opinion.

CAPTAIN

For my part, I had rather your appetite had wished for our good fellowship; for I had rather drink a health, then read a Copy of Verses; the truth is, I cannot endure Verses.

WILL

But if they were a Copy made in your Mistress praise you would like them.

CAPTAIN

I should hate my Mistress, throw the hate to the Verses, were she never so worthy, or the Verses so witty.

WILL

That makes thee love mean common Women.

CAPTAIN

They are fools that will wooe a nice Lady with flattering Verses, when they may have a free Wench, with plain Prose; and as the old saying, Jone in the dark is as good as my Lady.

HARRY

Nay faith, but they are not; for all common Wenches are unwholsome Sluts.

WILL

Well, leaving Jone and a Lady at this present, I would have you read a drunken Song, which I made to sing between every glass, for singing dries the Throat, and drought requires drink, all which will make us drink with more gust, and the wine will tast the quicker.

CAPTAIN

Faith, I hate verse so much, as the Song will make me vomit up my drink, besides singing brings down rhume, and to have salt rhume mixt with sharp wine, will cause such an unpleasing tast, which will make us more sick then Crocus Mettallorum, and spoile the wine; wherefore burn your Song; besides, let me tell you, as your friend, that 'tis very dangerous for a Drunkard to be a Poet; for the vapour of Wit, and the vapour of Wine, joyned together, will overpower your brain, and may make a man so mad, as to be past recovery; but when the brain is only muddl'd with the vapour of drink, sleep cures it, and drink causes sleep; whereas Poetry banishes sleep from the Sences, and heats the brain into a Fever.

WILL

But the hotter the brain is, the quicker the Wit is, and Poets drink Wine to heighten their fancy.

CAPTAIN

Let me tell you, Poets drink Wine to please their Pallats; and it is an old Saying, That when Drink is in, then Wit is out; wherefore burn thy Verses.

HARRY
Do, Will, take his Counsel, and burn them.

WILL
I will follow your advice, and burn them to light a pipe of Tobacco.

CAPTAIN
That is worse then if you should read them, or sing them; for you will suck them back into your brain, with the smoak, through your Pipe, and so have your Verses to return smoking hot, which will either smother your brain, or give your brain such an appetite, as you will never leave versifying. But come let us go and consult how they may be destroyed.

WILL
Content.

[Enter **PEG**.

CAPTAIN
Peg, have a care, and stay at home.

[Enter **MRS JANE FULLWIT**, **MRS ANNE SENCIBLE**, to **MRS PEG VALOROSA**, who walked in a Melancholy posture.

ANNE
Always Melancholy?

PEG
Who can be merry, that is poor?

JANE
Who lives more merry then Beggars?

PEG
But our Birth and Breeding will not suffer us to beg.

JANE
No, but we may live by our Wits.

PEG
But Wit was kill'd in the War.

ANNE
You are mistaken, it was only banished with the Cavaliers; but now it is returned home.

PEG

I cannot perceive it; for though I see many Fools, yet not a true natural Wit amongst them; for there is the Rhiming-fools, the Intrigue-fools, and the fine-languaged fools.

JANE
The truth is, the multitude of Fools obscure the Wits, like dark Clouds that obscure the Sun; but let us endeavour to shine through those Clouds.

PEG
That cannot be.

JANE
Let us try for our profit.

PEG
But Word-Wit will not make us rich.

JANE
I grant it, but Deed-Wit will do us good, wherefore let us endeavour to get rich Husbands.

PEG
We may endeavour it, but not obtain it.

ANNE
But if we could get them by our ingenuity, we know not where they are to be had.

JANE
Madam Informer will give us Intelligence.

[Enter **HARRY**.

HARRY
Is your Brother within the House?

JANE
I think he is, I will go and see.

[Exeunt **WOMEN**.

[Enter **WILL FULLWIT**.

HARRY
Well, I shall never trust any man more for your sake, nor never believe in Friendship.

WILL
Why?

HARRY

Do you ask why, when you who I did believe was so true a friend, would never forsake me at a time of need, when not only my Life, but my Honour was engaged in a quarrel, for which I chose you for my second, and then to fail me at the appointed time, was base; for had you been my Enemy, your Honour should have brought you into the field.

WILL
Faith, I was so engaged in a Company of Ladies, I could not come.

HARRY
Can there be a greater engagement then Friendship, Honour and Honesty?

WILL
Can there be a greater friendship then the love of Women, or more honourable then to serve the Female sex? and as for honesty, 'tis not worth any thing, besides, it is a fool, it brings a Man to ruine, at least a Man can never thrive by it.

HARRY
O judgment, how hath it erred, to chuse a Knave for a Friend, a Coward for a Second!

WILL
So I perceive, rather then you will want an Enemy, you will quarrel with your own judgment, you had best fight a Duel with that.

HARRY
Go, go, and kiss a Mistress, and leave talking of Duels.

WILL
I marry, this is friendly advice; for in Kisses there is life and pleasure, in Duels death and danger; but let me tell thee, Harry, I have done thee a more friendly part, in not appearing, then ever I did thee in my life; for I have saved thy life, at least thy estate, and have kept thy Honour pure and free from stains, and I have increast thy honour.

HARRY
Which way?

WILL
Thus; I have let thee go into thee Field for thy Honour, and have kept thine Enemy out, not by force, but by perswasion; which perswasion hath so wrought on him and his Second, as they will both meet in the same place you quarrel'd in, where shall be the same Company that drank, and was drunk there, and before that Company he will confess his fault, and ask pardon, which is as much satisfaction as an honest or honourable Man can desire; and it would be against the Laws of good fellowship to fight a sober Duel, for a drunken quarrel; wherefore agree, and be friends with our drunken Comrade.

[Enter **CAPTAIN**, **CORNET**, **LIEUTENANT**, and **DICK TRAVELLER**.

CAPTAIN
We heard you very high in words, I hope you two dear friends will not quarrel?

WILL
We shall not quarrel like Enemies; but Harry is angry, because I will not let him fight.

CAPTAIN
Fight, with whom will he fight?

WILL
With Tom Ranter.

LIEUTENANT
Hang him, he will get no honour with fighting with him.

CAPTAIN
Come, come, I will conduct you to a better pastime then fighting vain Duels; for there are a Company of Ladies which I am acquainted with, that have made a merry meeting, only they want Men to keep them Company.

WILL
Let us go; come Harry, will you go?

HARRY
Yes, with all my heart.

[Enter **PEG**.

CAPTAIN
I will but speak a word to my Sister.

[Exit **CAPTAIN**.

[He Whispers.

[**PEG** stands as if she were Musing.

[Enter **JANE** and **ANNE**.

ANNE
What are you thinking of now?

PEG
I was reasoning with my self, why those Women that was neither factious, ambitious, covetous, malicious nor cruel, should suffer in the Wars with the men.

JANE
The gods would not be just, if the Women did not suffer for the Crimes of the Men, since all Men suffer for a single crime of a particular woman, witness our Grandmother Eve.

[Enter **MADAM INFORMER**.

ANNE
O Madam Informer, have you made an Inquiry?

INFORMER
Yes, marry have I, and find the Mass of Wealth is in the possession of Usurers, Lawyers and Physicians.

JANE
I believe Usurers and Lawyers may be very rich, for the Civil War hath made those sorts of Men like as Vultures, after a Battel, that feed on the Dead, or dying Corps; but I cannot perceive why Physicians should be the richer for those times.

INFORMER
There is great reason why they should gain the more; for both Men and Womens bodies are corrupted, and weakned with Melancholy, Grief, Malice, Revenge, Envy, Wrong, Injustice, and the like; so that their bodies are full of the Scurvy, which their Misfortunes hath bred.

PEG
But have you found amongst these rich sorts of Men, any Widowers, or Batchelors?

INFORMER
Yes, that I have, three Batchelors; the richest amongst them, is one Mr. Get-all an Usurer; the other Serjeant Plead-all a Lawyer; the third Doctor Cure-all a Physician.

JANE
Which is the richest?

INFORMER
The Usurer; for he is worth Two hundred thousand Pounds.

PEG
Well, we will imploy our Wits to get these Men.

INFORMER
But Wit without Assistance, will do no good; wherefore you must get your Brothers, and their Friends to help you by their industry.

JANE
Your Counsel is good.

[Exeunt,—only Peg meets her Brother, Captain, as coming in.

PEG
Brother, are you well, you look so Melancholy?

CAPTAIN
In body, but not in mind, Peg.

[Exit **PEG**.

[Enter **WILL** and **HARRY**, the **CAPTAIN**, and the **REST**.

HARRY
Captain, what makes thee so sad?

CAPTAIN
That which would make any Man sad, want of Money.

WILL
We may be as sad as you for that; but to be poor and Melancholy is a double misery.

CAPTAIN
Life cannot be merry, when it hath not any thing to live upon.

[Enter **DICK TRAVELLER**.

CAPTAIN
Dick, where have you been?

DICK
I have been peeping through a Key-hole into a Room, where your three Sisters are in serious Councel with Madam Informer.

CAPTAIN
Pray God she is not instructing of them to be Wenches.

WILL
Faith, I fear it; for she would make an ingenuous Bawd.

CAPTAIN
I will go and part them.

DICK
Pray do not; for perchance the Womens Wits may do you more service then your own; for I heard them say, their Brothers must assist them; and surely they do not believe you would be their Pimps.

HARRY
No, for they know we shall rather be their Murtherers then their Pimps.

DICK
Then let them alone; and whilst they are in a Councel, let us go to the Tavern and drink.

CAPTAIN
But we have no Money.

DICK

I have a little credit to run on the Score.

HARRY
Faith, if we go to the Tavern, the Girls will come crying after us.

DICK
I tell you they are so busie about some Female-design, as they will not miss us.

[Exeunt **ALL** but the **CORNET**.

CORNET
I must stay to tell a lie, because they shall not follow us.

[Enter **PEG**, **JANE**, and **ANNE**.

CORNET
Ladies, your Brothers bid me tell you, they are gone about some serious business; but they will return soon.

PEG
When they will.

[Exit **CORNET**.

[Enter **INFORMER**.

PEG
Mrs. Informer, how shall we three agree in the choice of the three Rich Men?

INFORMER
You must draw Lots, and I have made them ready.

JANE
I pray Jupiter, I may draw the Rich Man.

ANNE
I pray Jupiter, I may draw him.

PEG
We must take our Lot, let it be what it will.

[**JANE** draws first.

[They Draw.

INFORMER
Which have you drawn?

JANE

I have drawn Serjeant Plead-all.

[**ANNE SENCIBLE** draws.

ANNE

I have drawn Doctor Cure-all.

PEG

Jove, I thank thee in giving the Usurer to me.

INFORMER

Now go to your Brothers, and inform them of your designs.

JANE

Faith, they will rather laugh at us, then help us.

ANNE

But yet we dare not do any such thing without their knowledge.

PEG

I am confident my Brother will assist me.

JANE

Come, let us go to them.

[Exeunt.

SCENE V

[Enter **CAPTAIN**, **HARRY**, **WILL**, **DICK**, **LIEUTENANT** and **CORNET**; as in the Tavern.

WILL

Well, this Wine is so fresh and full of Spirit, as it would make a Fool a Poet.

HARRY

Or a Poet a Fool.

DICK

Then here's a Health to the most Fools in the World.

CAPTAIN

Then you must drink a Health to the whole World, that is one great Fool.

LIEUTENANT

Prithee Dick do not drink that Health, for it will choak thee; for the World of Fools is too big for one Draught.

DICK
Then here's a Health to the wisest Man.

CORNET
You may as well drink a Health to a drop of water in the Ocean.

CAPTAIN
Faith Dick, that health is so little, it cannot be tasted; besides, I do not love droppings.

DICK
Then here's a Health to the Honest'st man in the World.

WILL
That Health is more difficult then the last? for it is as rare to know an Honest man, as to see a Phoenix.

DICK
Then I will drink a Health to the Chastest Woman.

LIEUTENANT
You might as well drink a Health to the Queen of the Faries, which is an old Wives-tale; for Chastity lives only in the Name not in Nature.

DICK
Then here's a Health to a Common Courtesan.

HARRY
A Pox of that Health, I will not pledge it.

WILL
Then here's a Health to the Muses.

CAPTAIN
It is a shame for a Soldier to drink a Health to the Muses.

LIEUTENANT
The truth is, I hate a Poetical Soldier.

HARRY
Is it not lawful for a Soldier (Captain) to have Wit?

CAPTAIN
No; for Wit makes the minds of Men soft, sweet, gentle, and effeminate; insomuch as those that have Wit, are not fit for Soldiers; for Soldiers should have resolute minds, cloudy thoughts, hard hearts, rough speeches, and boisterous actions.

CORNET
The truth is (Captain) there is as much difference between a Poet and a Soldier (which is Wit and Courage) as between a Calm and a Storm.

CAPTAIN
You say true, Cornet; for certainly the best Soldiers are born and bred in the uncivillest Nations.

LIEUTENANT
No doubt of it, Captain.

DICK
Then here's a Health to the Graces.

CAPTAIN
That Health is three times worse then the former, which was nine times too bad; for when did you know a Soldier to have Grace?

LIEUTENANT
The truth is (Captain) it is unnatural for a Soldier to have Grace.

CAPTAIN
You say true, Lieutenant.

WILL
Setting aside, the Muses and the Graces, here is a Health to the Furies.

CAPTAIN
I marry Sir, that Health sounds like a Soldier's
Health, and I will pledge it were the Glass full of
Wounds. Here Harry, here's the Furies Health.

HARRY
Faith, Captain, we shall be furiously drunk with the Furies Health.

CORNET
It will give fire to your brain.

HARRY
Yes, and burn out my Reason.

[They Drink.

CAPTAIN
Now I will begin another Health; Here Gentlemen, here is Death's Health.

DICK

Good Captain, do not drink Death's Health, for it will make our Wine so cold it will never warm us; besides, dead Wine will never make us drunk; and if we had not a desire to be drunk, we should not have come to now the Tavern.

CAPTAIN
Dick, you must drink Death's Health, for Death's Health will make you dead drunk.

DICK
Then I will drink it, and invite you and the rest of the Society to my Funeral.

CAPTAIN
Then we will carry thee to thy bed with Ceremony, as to thy Grave, sounding a dead March with empty Pots, trayling our Tobacco-pipes instead of Pikes, and spew out Wine instead of Tears.

[Enter **PEG**, **JANE**, and **ANNE**, as to the Tavern.

HARRY
Did not I tell you they would come.

CAPTAIN
What come you for now?

JANE
Not to complain or chide, but to desire your assistance to our Designs.

WILL
Let your Tongues and Tayls assist you.

PEG
No, our Wits and Honesty shall assist us.

CAPTAIN
Pray Jove you have either.

HARRY
Well, let us hear your Designs.

ANNE
It is to get us Rich Husbands.

CAPTAIN
Sister Peg, tell me truly, is the Design so honest, and honourable as only to get a Rich Husband.

PEG
There is no deceit in the end, but only in the way or means.

CAPTAIN
Come, let us go, for perchance our Sister's honest Wits may get us Honourable Means to live with.

[Exeunt.

[Enter **LADY**, and her **SECOND SUITER**.

SUITER
Madam, I was here some little while ago, to tender my duty to you; but hearing you were not in a pleasing humour, I durst not venture to present my Suit, for there is a nick of Time for Lovers to speed.

LADY
Sir, I perceive you are well learned in old Observations.

SUITER
As for Learning of all kinds and sorts, I defie it, in so much that I cannot read the Horn-book; neither am I able to remember the relation of any Discourse, if there be words in it that consist but of two Sillables.

LADY
How will you make Love then?

SUITER
Thus Madam, I love you with all my heart.

LADY
What Jointure will you make me?

SUITER
Love.

LADY
What maintenance will you give me?

SUITER
Love.

LADY
Can Love feed, Cloth and maintain me?

SUITER
Love is the true Elixir, and above all price, being above Gold; it is a Creator, Madam.

LADY
If your Love be a Creator, then my Love shall be your Creature.

[Exit **LADY**, **SUITER** Solus.

SUITER
The Devil himself cannot work upon a Womans Nature.

[Enter the **LADY**, and a **THIRD SUITER**.

SUITER
Madam, I hear you are Rich.

LADY
What then Sir?

SUITER
And I am poor.

LADY
What then?

SUITER
Therefore I desire you would be pleased to marry me.

LADY
For what?

SUITER
To mend my Fortune.

LADY
I am no Cobler, Sir.

[Exit **LADY**, **SUITER** Solus.

SUITER
The Devil take Women's Tongues, for they make Men Fools.

ACT III

SCENE I

[Enter **HARRY**, and **DOCTOR CURE-ALL**.

HARRY
Doctor Cure-all, hearing of your fame, hath caused me to fend for you, to assist me with your help.

DOCTOR CURE-ALL
What is your Disease?

HARRY

That you must tell me; but my pain lies in my bones.

DOCTOR CURE-ALL

I understand your Disease; you must be put to a diet, and you must sweat, and bathe, and something else, if need require it.

HARRY

I hope I have not the Pox, Doctor?

DOCTOR CURE-ALL

You may say it is a Cold, or so; but do you not feel a tenderness in your Nose, or a weakness in your Legs?

HARRY

My Legs are somewhat weak.

DOCTOR CURE-ALL

Do you spit much?

HARRY

Sometimes, but not much.

DOCTOR CURE-ALL

It were well if you did; for that Evacuation is good for young Men.

[Gives him a Fee.

DOCTOR CURE-ALL

By no means Sir.

HARRY

Pray Doctor take it.

DOCTOR CURE-ALL

Well Sir, I shall prescribe some Remedies.

HARRY

I shall come to your House, and Visit you sometimes, Doctor.

DOCTOR CURE-ALL

You shall be welcome Sir; if I am not mistaken, your Name is Mr. Sencible.

HARRY

It is so Sir, your Servant Doctor.

[Exit **DOCTOR**.

[Enter **CAPTAIN** and **WILL** to **HARRY**.

CAPTAIN
Harry, it seems you are sick, for we met the Doctor; but what says he to thee.

HARRY
He says, I have the Pox.

WILL
A Plague of him, but he hath the Money.

HARRY
I lent him two Pieces upon Interest.

CAPTAIN
For the hopes of thy Cure: But Will Fullwit, have you got your Sister into the Serjeant's service?

WILL
Yes, and he likes her Service very well.

CAPTAIN
But Harry, how doth your Sisters design go on?

HARRY
Faith slowly; for this is the first time I ever saw the Doctor, but I hope it will come to a good issue in time; but how far is your Sisters design gone?

CAPTAIN
So far as I am almost ready to summon him to a Spiritual Court, and yet I have neither spoke to, nor seen the Usurer Get-all; but when a business is well laid,
it is half done.

HARRY
But if it be to appear before the Spiritual Court, it will be cast forth.

CAPTAIN
I will warrant you I shall get such a Judg, as will end the cause on my side; but both of you must be assistants; wherefore let us go to Dick Traveller, where we shall meet my Lieutenant, and Cornet, whom I have well instructed.

[Enter **DICK**, **LIEUTENANT** and **CORNET**.

CAPTAIN
O, you have prevented us; are you ready for the design?

DICK
Yes.

CAPTAIN
But do you understand the cause well?

DICK
So well as I shall not need any further Instruction; but where's my Fee?

CAPTAIN
But stay, the Cause is not ended; for though a Bribe go before, a Fee comes after.

LIEUTENANT
If Judges and Lawyers should not be Fee'd before Causes were decided, they would not be so rich as they are; but Doctors usually have their Fees after their Prescriptions and Advice; wherefore, Will Fullwit, that must be; Doctor Feel-pulse must not be fee'd before hand.

CAPTAIN
I only fear Will is not learned enough to play the part of a Doctor of Physick.

WILL
Never fear me, for I shall out-argue the Colledge.

DICK
Harry, and your Lieutenant, and Cornet must act as under Officers and Clerks.

CAPTAIN
Let Harry act the part of a Clerk, and leave us to be under Officers.

CAPTAIN
No, no, Harry must be a Pleader; but I never thought Soldiers should turn Judges, and Lawyers before now.

DICK
Why not as well as Priests turn Soldiers.

CAPTAIN
Come, let us go about this great affair.

[Enter **PEG**.

CAPTAIN
Peg, have you got your Child ready?

PEG
Yes.

WILL
Have you Confidence to outface the Court?

PEG
I can face the Court; but I fear I cannot outface or out-case the Usurer Get-all.

CAPTAIN
Never fear it, Peg.

PEG
Pray Jove we speed, for the good of the Common-wealth of Cavaliers.

CAPTAIN
Well Peg, be ready against I send for you.

[Exeunt **MEN**.

[Enter **ANNE**, and **INFORMER**, to **PEG**.

ANNE
How is your Design like to prove?

PEG
Well I hope; but Mrs. Informer, have you seen
Jane Fullwit since she went to be a Lawyer's Clerk?

INFORMER
I have, and she told me, that her Master is much pleased with her service; but I going often to visit his Clerk, the Serjeant having notice of it watched when I was with him, and was very angry, and said I was such a Bawd as corrupted all the Apprentices, and Lawyer's Clerks in the City. But I fear for all your industry, your Designs will not come to that effect you desire.

PEG
Why, what hinders them?

INFORMER
Why, those three rich men, that I informed you of, do eagarly wooe the old Lady Riches.

JANE
Are the men young, or old?

INFORMER
Neither; they are of a middle age.

ANNE
Then she will never marry any of them; for old Women love young Men; besides, she can marry but one.

PEG
Come, come, it is impossible, but we shall be preferred before the old Lady.

INFORMER

I wish you may.

PEG
I will warrant you, we shall have good success if you act your part well.

INFORMER
Never fear me, for I shall out-act you all.

PEG
Come, let us go to the Child, to put a dry Cloath to it, and to wrap it warm with a Mantle, for fear it catch cold; for if it get Cold, my Brother will be angry.

[Exit **WOMEN**.

[**GET-ALL** the Usurer sitting casting up Accounts, Enter his Man **ROGER**.

ROGER
Will your Worship give me leave to speak freely to you?

GET-ALL
Yes, Roger, freely.

ROGER
I wonder your Worship will starve your life, to fill your Purse.

GET-ALL
O Roger, when the Purse is full, the life cannot starve for want.

ROGER
'Tis true, he that is Rich may eat if he have a Stomack; but you will neither eat nor sleep, but wear out your life in casting up the Accounts of your Riches, and yet have not an Heir to leave it to.

GET-ALL
Wealth never wants Heirs.

ROGER
Indeed such Heirs, that will give no thanks for what they do receive?

GET-ALL
But I can make the Meritorious my Heirs.

ROGER
You may make Heirs, but not Merit, Sir.

GET-ALL
Do you think there are not Men of Merit?

ROGER

Faith Sir, Merit died many years since, and left no Posterity.

[Enter **TOM** his other Man.

TOM
Sir, there is one Captain Valour desires to speak with your Worship.

GET-ALL
These poor Cavaliers haunt me like Spirits, they will not let me rest in peace.

ROGER
Faith Sir, they are like Hounds, that hunt an after-Game.

GET-ALL
But they shall not catch my Wealth; for they have no Lands to Mortgage, nor Goods to Pawn.

ROGER
I believe they have not any thing to pawn or Mortgage, unless it be their Honesties.

GET-ALL
But poor Honesty will pay no Debts; wherefore tell the Captain, I am not to be spoken with.

[Exit **TOM**.

ROGER
But your Worship said, you would leave your Wealth to Men of Merit.

GET-ALL
Yes, Roger, I may leave them my Wealth when I die; but not give it them whilst I live.

ROGER
But if the Cavaliers be Men of Merit, they may be starved before you are like to die; for you are not fifty years of age, and healthful and temperate, whereas they are weak with want and disorders.

GET-ALL
Want and disorders seldom go together; wherefore we'l endeavour to get the old Lady Riches.

ROGER
What, to be disorderly?

GET-ALL
No, to be Rich.

ROGER
But would you Marry this old Lady Riches in earnest?

GET-ALL

Yes; but I would not see her before I am Married, for fear I should dislike her; and that would disquiet my mind between two Passions, Dislike and Covetousness.

ROGER
But you have a Mass of Wealth already, so in my judgment you should desire no more.

GET-ALL
You are a Fool; for I would be as Rich as the Indies, and then I should be more then half as Rich as the King of Spain.

ROGER
But what would you do with it, if you had it?

GET-ALL
I would fight with the Great Turk.

ROGER
But you said, That you would give your Wealth to Men of Merit.

GET-ALL
Why so I shall, if I give it to Valiant Soldiers, to fight against the Turk.

ROGER
But would your Worship head your own Army?

GET-ALL
Yes.

ROGER
Truly that would be a kind of a Miracle; for I never heard of an Usurer that was Valiant.

[Enter the **TOM** the Servant again.

TOM
Sir, Captain Valour is without still, he will not go away.

GET-ALL
I cannot speak with him.

TOM
He bids me tell you, That he doth not come to borrow Money, for he knows you will lend him none; but he says, He came to inform you of a business that highly concerns you.

GET-ALL
Well, bring him in; but be sure Roger and Tom, that both of you be in the next room, for I do not love to be with a Soldier alone.

ROGER

But you dare trust your self at the head of an Army.

GET-ALL
Yes, yes, but that is against the Turk; but hold your prating and send in the Captain.

[Exit **ROGER**.

[Enter **CAPTAIN**.

CAPTAIN
Mr. Get-all, I am come to inform you, that there is a young Gentlewoman brought to bed.

GET-ALL
What is that to me.

CAPTAIN
It is to you, if it be true what they say, which is, that you got it.

GET-ALL
If she can prove I got it, I will not only keep the Child, but marry the Woman; but I did believe I was always insufficient.

CAPTAIN
You speak as an honest Gentleman, and I shall tell her what you say.

[Exit **CAPTAIN**.

[Enter **ROGER**.

GET-ALL
Roger, I am provided of an Heir, for I have a Child laid to my Charge.

ROGER
Of the Captain 's begetting.

GET-ALL
I believe so; but the Wench lays it to my charge.

ROGER
Faith Sir, I never saw any thing like a Woman, near your Worship, since I came to be your Servant, which is above Twenty years; as for your old Cook-maid, she is nothing like a Woman.

GET-ALL
Why, what is she like then?

ROGER
Like a Spirit, whose substance is wasted in Hell-fire.

GET-ALL

Well Roger, but I must be careful to avoid this Wenches plot against me, and there is no way, that I can perceive, to avoid it, but to marry as speedily as I can; wherefore carry the old Lady Riches that Present, and let her into my Chamber, and if it be possible speak to her self and wooe her for me.

ROGER

Faith Sir, I am as bad a wooer as your self; for I never wooed any Woman but your Cook-maid for a Breakfast, or to make me a Bag-pudding; and how such kind of Wooing will fit a Lady, I cannot tell.

GET-ALL

But you can tell her, how Rich I am.

ROGER

That I can, and in my Conscience that is as good a wooing-Plea as any is.

GET-ALL

And you may tell her that one of my age is fitter to match with one of her age, then a younger man.

ROGER

Those two Arguments will spoile all, especially that of mentioning her age, for Women cannot endure to hear of their age, were they as old as Methuselah.

GET-ALL

Well, use what Arguments you shall think fit.

ROGER

Shall I Wooe as the young Gallants, in Court Language?

GET-ALL

What Language is that?

ROGER

Fine Phrases, and Mode-expressions, which is a mixture with French words, and high Complements.

GET-ALL

How high?

ROGER

As high as Non-sence, which is beyond Understanding.

GET-ALL

Prithee use what Language or Expressions you will.

ROGER

But put the case I should wooe so courtly, as to get her for my self?

GET-ALL

If you do Roger, I shall wish you joy.

ROGER
I thank you Sir.

[Exit **ROGER**.

[Enter **TOM** his other Man.

TOM
Sir, there is a young Gentlewoman come in a Coach, who desires to speak with your Worship.

GET-ALL
I'le pawn my life it is she, that desires to lay her Bastard to my Charge.

TOM
Certainly, she is none of that trade, for she is come in a Coach.

GET-ALL
Why a Hackney Woman may ride in a Hackney-Coach; there is no Law against it, Tom.

TOM
But in my conscience this Gentlewoman looks as modestly, as if she were honest.

GET-ALL
But a modest Countenance is oftentimes made use of only to cover the face of Adultery.

TOM
Then you will not speak with her?

GET-ALL
No, for there is Antipathy between me and
Women-kind, since this Accusation.

[**TOM** was going out, and returns back.

TOM
Sir, here is the Captain.

[Enter **CAPTAIN**.

GET-ALL
What would you have now?

CAPTAIN
I am come to summon you to the Spiritual Court.

GET-ALL
I shall obey; but how shall I find the Court, for I was never there?

CAPTAIN
I will go but to the next house to speak with a friend, and I will come and direct you to the place.

GET-ALL
I pray do.

[Exit **CAPTAIN**.

[Enter **ROGER**.

GET-ALL
I am glad you are not gone to the Lady, for I am summoned to the Spiritual Court.

ROGER
The Captain 's coming made me stay, but what are you summoned for, a bag of Money?

GET-ALL
Indeed that is the design, but the pretence is, for getting the Child, I told you was laid to my Charge.

ROGER
Why, this is the misery of Wealth, a man can never be quiet; and you being very rich, it will be the policy of the Spiritual Court, to make you maintain all the Whores, and their Bastards, in the City.

GET-ALL
Like enough.

ROGER
And if there be an overplus, you may leave that to the Meritorious; so then you will maintain Vice in your life, and Virtue when you are dead.

GET-ALL
But surely my Innocency will defend me from the injury of Injustice.

ROGER
Faith, Injustice is too prevalent for Innocency, in these days.

GET-ALL
Well, let us go, for I must obey the Laws.

ROGER
But Sir, you are not provided of Lawyers to Plead on your side.

GET-ALL
I shall not need them, for I can declare my own Innocency.

[Exeunt **GET-ALL** and **SERVANT**.

[Enter as in a Court of Justice; **DICK**, as prime Judge of the Spiritual Court, the **LIEUTENANT** and **CORNET** as two Clerks, **HARRY SENCIBLE** as a Lawyer, or Pleader, for the Plaintiff; **WILL FULLWIT** as a Physician; **MRS PEG VALOROSA** the Plaintiff; **INFORMER**, as a Midwife and Witness; and **CAPTAIN VALOROUS** as their Friend; when all sit in Order.

[Enter **GET-ALL** and **ROGER**.

HARRY
Most Reverend Judge, here is a Gentlewoman come, who desires Justice.

DICK
What is her Cause?

HARRY
Her Cause is, That she being a virtuous young Woman, hath behaved her self modestly, and hath kept a good Reputation in the World (which all her Neighbours know) until such time as this Mr. Get-all got her with Child, which Child he will neither own nor keep, nor marry the Woman.

DICK
Have you any Witnesses?

HARRY
We have such a Witness as the Law allows of, which is a Midwife.

GET-ALL
I require the Witness to be heard.

DICK
Will you witness that the Child is Mr. Get-all 's.

INFORMER
I will witness the words of the Labouring Woman.

DICK
Declare them.

INFORMER
About Twelve a Clock at Night I being in bed, and fast asleep, there comes a Man, and raps, and raps, and—raps at the Door, as if it had been for life, which in truth proved so; for it was to fetch me to bring a sweet Babe into the World; but I hearing one rap so hard, I was afraid, my Door, being but a rotten Door, should be broke to pieces; I ran to the Window to ask, who knockt so hard, but the man knockt on, and I call'd out; which knocking and calling took up half an hours time; but at last, my Tongue being louder then the Clapper, he heard me then; I asked him what was his business? he said, I must go presently to a young Gentlewoman that was in Labour; upon which summons I did rise and put on my Bodise, but did not half lace them; also my Petticoats, but did not tie them fast enough; for when I came into the middle of the broad Street, my Coats fell quite down from my hips, but as good luck would have it, it was a dark Night, but the ill fortune was, that my Coats fell down, when I was striding over the

broad Kennel, in which posture I stood a great time, until the man helpt me over; but my Coats were all wet.

GET-ALL
But what is all this to the Confession of the Labouring Woman?

[She answers angerly.

INFORMER
It is of concern; for Circumstance is partly a declaring of truth.

DICK
You say true Mistress, wherefore go on.

INFORMER
But as I said—stay, I have forgot; where did I leave?

CAPTAIN
You left at the wet Coats, Mistress.

INFORMER
'Tis very true, I humbly thank you Sir; The Coats, as I said, being wet, I was loth to put them on, not only for fear of catching cold, but for fear I should endanger the Womans miscarriage by my retardments; so I went with never a Coat on me, the Man carried them for me; but the night was pretty warm, so that I got no Cold, I thank Jupiter; but being more nimble, as being more light, I was soon at the house of the Labouring Woman, whom I found in painful throws, and she groaned most pitifully; and I comforted her, and prayed her to have patience, and at last she was brought to bed of a very lusty Boy.

GET-ALL
But what did the Gentlewoman confess?

INFORMER
What Gentlewoman?

GET-ALL
This Gentlewoman.

INFORMER
This Gentlewoman hath confest that she was never got with Child, nor never had a Child, but what Mr. Get-all begot; and this I will take my Oath of.

DICK
How can you clear your self Mr. Get-all?

GET-ALL
I will take my Oath that I never did see this Gentlewoman, about whom I am accused, in my life; and I have a Servant here that can witness for me.

[**ROGER** comes forward.

DICK
What can you witness?

ROGER
I can witness that I have lived with my Master these Twenty years, in all which time I did never see my Master converse with any thing like a Woman.

DICK
Doth your Master keep no Servant-Maid?

ROGER
There is one we call the Cook-maid, but whether she be Maid or Woman, I'le take my Oath I know not.

DICK
Then your Master may converse with Women you know not of.

ROGER
But I will swear my Master did never converse with this Gentlewoman that hath the Child.

GET-ALL
And I will take my Oath, as I said, that I never did so much as see her before now.

CAPTAIN
But may it please you, most Reverend Judge, this Gentlewoman hath seen him.

GET-ALL
But the bare sight of me could not get her with Child.

CAPTAIN
That is to be proved; wherefore we require so much justice of this Reverend Judge, that Mr. Feel-pulse, a most learned and expert Doctor of Physick, may prove it by Argumentation.

DICK
Let Mr. Doctor prove it.

[**WILL** steps forward.

WILL
Then be it known to this most Reverend Judge, and to Mr. Get-all, and the rest of this Assembly, That our Famous Doctor is of opinion, (as also the heads of our Schools and Colledges) That the production of Animal kind, is by an Incorporeal motion; and the famous Doctor is also of opinion, That the Soul of Man slides from the Stomack to the heel, and in that journey makes a production: And all the Platonicks do affirm, That there may be a Conjunction of Souls, although the Bodies be at a far distance; and I am absolutely of that opinion; and that the Idea of a Man, by the help of a strong imagination, may beget a Child; which is sufficiently proved; for she seeing Mr. Get-all enter into the house of Mr. Inkhorn the

Scrivener, viewed his person so exactly, that when she was in bed, a strong imagination seized on her, by which she conceived a Child.

GET-ALL
It seems the Child was begot like the Plague, by conceit.

DICK
You say true, Mr. Get-all; wherefore you must marry the Woman, own the Child, and keep them both.

GET-ALL
Is there no avoiding your Sentence, Mr. Judge?

JUDGE
No, the Decree is past.

GET-ALL
Why then as she was got with Child by
Conceit, so I will marry her by Conceit.

JUDGE
But you must take her, and her Child home, and maintain them.

GET-ALL
Cannot I maintain them by Conceit?

JUDGE
No, that must be done Corporally.

GET-ALL
If there be no remedy, I must be content; come my Conceited or Platonick Wife and Child, let us go home.

OMNES
We wish you all Happiness.

[Exeunt.

SCENE II

[Enter the **LADY** and a **FOURTH SUITER**.

SUITER
Madam I suppose my Name is unknown to you?

LADY
'Tis probable Sir; for I never saw you before.

SUITER
Then I'le tell you, Madam, my Name is, Monsieur Vanity.

LADY
Your Name shews that your Humour is Foolish, and your actions Prodigal.

SUITER
My Humour is noble, Madam, and my Actions generous; for I usually cast away a hundred pounds at Dice, and run away a hundred pounds at a Race, and give away a hundred pounds at a Visit to a Mistress.

LADY
This last kind of Prodigality has some resemblance to Generosity; but yet it is as different from Generosity, as a Bribe is from an Uninteressed Gift. But pray Sir, give me leave to ask you, what design brought you hither to me?

SUITER
A very good design, Madam; for I being vain, and you rich, 'twould be very convenient we two should joyn as Man and Wife, that one might maintain the other.

LADY
Alas Sir, the Wife would soon die in her Husbands arms; for Riches consume in Vanity; therefore, I will as soon marry death, as you.

[Exit **LADY**.

SUITER [Solus]
Death take her, if I cannot get her.

[Enter **THREE GENTLEWOMEN** to the **LADY**.

LADY
I am glad you are come to release me from the importunity of my Suiters.

1ST GENTLEWOMAN
You are in a good Condition, Madam, that you can have Lovers that seek you, when as we for want of Wealth, are forced to seek them.

2ND GENTLEWOMAN
You mean Husbands, Madam, for Lovers are never sought, because they are never lost; for a Lover will always be at the tayl of his Mistress.

3RD GENTLEWOMAN
I wish I had as many as would make up a Train.

[Exit **SUITER**.

[Enter her Father **SAVE-ALL**.

FATHER
Daughter, have you made your choice of a
Husband, since you have so many Suiters?

DAUGHTER
No truly Sir, for the number confounds my choice, or rather there is no choice in all the number, by
reason none exceeds the other, but they are all Fools alike.

FATHER
Indeed Daughter, if you be so long a chusing, you will be past choice your self.

DAUGHTER
I had rather be old with Judgment, then young with Folly; and since you have been pleased to trust to
my discretion, I would not willingly betray that trust, by the hast of my choice.

FATHER
You speak well, Daughter; Heaven grant you do well.

DAUGHTER
But pray Sir give me leave to ask you one question.

FATHER
What's that?

DAUGHTER
I would fain know, whether my Lovers do first address their Suits to you, or to me?

FATHER
Their Suites they address first to you; but their inquiries are made first to me; to wit, what Portion I
would give you, and whether I intend to settle all my Estate upon you.

DAUGHTER
It seems they consider my Wealth before my Person.

FATHER
Yes, and all Wooers do the like.

DAUGHTER
But not Lovers Sir.

FATHER
Yes, yes, for they wooe first, marry next, and love last.

[Exit **FATHER**.

[Enter the **FIFTH SUITER** to the **LADY**, being an ancient Man.

SUITER
Madam, I see you are a Beauty, and Report speaks you Virtuous and Wise; which if so, I hope you'l chuse an ancient Lover before a young one.

LADY
No question Sir, but an ancient Lover expresses more Constancy in his Love, then a young one doth; but ancient Love requires a great deal of time, and my Father may die before I make my Choice.

SUITER
You mistake me, Madam, I mean an ancient Man that loves you.

LADY
There is great difference between an ancient Man, and an ancient Lover: But Sir, by your Discourse I perceive you pretend to be a Lover.

SUITER
My Love is not pretended; for I do really love you.

LADY
How can I know that?

SUITER
By proof; for I'le not require any Portion with you, since I am Rich enough without; Nay, I will not only take you without a Portion, but make you Mistress of all my Wealth, in so much that I will freely give you all I am Worth; and I wish I were worth Millions for your sake.

LADY
Sir, you express more Love in your Gifts,then all my young Suiters in their Words; and if you will confirm your Promise to my Father, which you have now made to me, I shall accept of you for a Husband, and promise you, to be an honest and Loving Wife.

[He Kisses her Hand.

SUITER
Let us both go to your Father, and conclude the bargain.

ACT IV

SCENE I

[Enter **LAWYER** and his Clerk, **JACK**.

SERJEANT

Is Doctor Cure-all so industrious about the old Lady Riches?

JACK

Yes Sir, he was very busie in preparing of Cordials, Ointments, and such things; and was angry that I came with a Message from you; for he bid me be gone; for the Lady, he said, could not hear Love-Messages, she was so full of Sciatical pain and Gout; but the old Lady did favour me, and chid the Doctor for bidding me to be gone; for she would have heard my Message, when her sides were anointed, and her Gouty Toe Plaistered.

SERJEANT

And did you stand by, till she was anointed?

JACK

Yes Sir, for she did desire me to help to anoint her sides, whilst the Doctor laid a Plaister to her Toe.

SERJEANT

And how did she like your service?

JACK

So well, Sir, as she said, she was never better chaft and rubbed in her life; I suppose it was for your sake.

SERJEANT

But when I am married, I shall not allow her my Clerk to anoint her sides, although she be so old to go upon Crutches.

[Exit **JACK**, Clerk.

[Enter another **CLERK**.

CLERK

Sir, there is a Client without, desires to speak with you; and there is a Gentleman without, that doth raile bitterly.

SERJEANT

For what?

CLERK

Because his Law-Suit went against him; he says, That all the poor Cavaliers are not only undone by the Wars, but also by the Lawyers.

SERJEANT

These poor Cavaliers are very troublesome.

MAN

Alass, their Losses make them impatient.

SERJEANT

They are so poor, that Lawyers cannot gain by them; wherefore, we are for the other Party, who are so rich, that 'tis fit their Purses should be emptied.

MAN

But if they get their Suites, Sir, the poor Cavaliers pay the Charges.

SERJEANT

Hold your prating, and bid Jack Clerk come to me.

[Enter **JACK** the Clerk.

SERJEANT

Have you writ those Deeds out?

JACK

Yes Sir.

SERJEANT

And have you Copied out those Cases that I am to plead for, and against?

JACK

Yes Sir.

SERJEANT

'Tis well done.

JACK

Sir, you are pleased to seem to favour me.

SERJEANT

I do really love thee, and will do thee any favour I can.

JACK

Then I desire you would be pleased to Plead a Cause that concerns a Kinswoman of mine.

SERJEANT

That I will to the best of my power; but what is the Case?

JACK

Why Sir, I have a Kinswoman who is well born, but poor, and a Gentlewoman; but a Gentleman being in Love with her, and she not condescending to his unlawful desire, hath taken her away by force, and keeps her by force.

SERJEANT

Have you Witness?

JACK

Yes Sir, I have two Witnesses.

SERJEANT
That is sufficient; let them be ready at the next Sessions.

JACK
But Sir, I desire not to appear as Plaintiff, for I have got another Gentleman to be Plaintiff; and my Friends are without, Sir, if you please to see them.

SERJEANT
Well, call them.

[Enter the **LIEUTENANT** and **CORNET**.

SERJEANT
Gentlemen, I shall serve you as well as I can.

LIEUTENANT & **CORNET**
We thank you Sir.

[Exit **SERJEANT**.

[Enter **DICK**, **WILL**, **HARRY** and **CAPTAIN**.

JACK
Gentlemen, you are welcome.

WILL
We are come to know if we shall have a Hearing?

JACK
My Master hath promised to Plead on our behalf.

HARRY
We desire no more.

JACK
But I am to inform this Society, That there is a very rich old Lady, (a Widow) who these three Rich Men court; The Usurer did Wooe her, and the Lawyer and Physician do Wooe her; now if any one of you could cozen these Three of the Lady, it would be a Master-piece.

HARRY
But should not any one of us cozen our selves, or she cozen us to marry her? for she is so old, that there is no hopes of Posterity.

DICK

Why shall we desire Posterity, so long as we are poor? and if any one of us should ever come to be so happy as to be Rich, if he hath no Children, and chance to die, let him leave his Wealth amongst the Society of poor Cavaliers.

ALL SPEAK
Content, content.

LIEUTENANT
But which of us shall address himself to this old Lady?

HARRY
Dick Traveller is most likely to speed.

DICK
I have white Hairs; wherefore I am confident I shall be refused.

CAPTAIN
The truth is, the only Man that is probable to speed, is Harry Sencible; for he hath a young smooth face, and old Women love young smooth fac'd Men alife.

HARRY
Yes, but a young Man doth not love an old Woman; wherefore she is a fitter match for Dick then for me.

WILL
Harry is in the right, Dick is the fittest Match for her; but the difficulty will be, how to make the Match, for we shall find it more difficult for all us Men to cozen one Woman, then for one Woman to cozen all us Men.

LIEUTENANT
It is impossible; wherefore let us never endeavour it.

CORNET
But we will never lose any design for want of endeavour.

JACK
I will tell you my Masters, how to compass this design.

DICK
How?

JACK
Harry shall put himself into a Woman's Habit, and Madam Informer who is acquainted with the Lady, shall prefer Harry to be her Chamber-Maid, where he may have time and opportunity to commend Dick, and to bring him acquainted with her.

WILL
He may do some good in that, and perchance not.

JACK
It is but trying.

HARRY
I like the design so well, as I am resolved to become a Chamber-Maid.

WILL
But we shall want thy Company in the mean time.

HARRY
No, no, I am confident I shall get leave sometimes to go abroad, or find some ways or other to slip out.

LIEUTENANT
But you cannot change your Habit suddenly.

HARRY
I shall not have occasion, for you all know me.

DICK
Come, come, let us about this business.

JACK
But first you must go with me to hear the Cause try'd.

ALL SPEAK
Content, content.

[Exeunt.

[Enter **ROGER**, Solus.

ROGER
If my young Mistress should have a perfect Idea of me, and then a strong Imagination, she might prove with Child again, and so my Master would be a Platonick Cuckold.

[Enter **GET-ALL**.

GET-ALL
Roger, where is my Platonick Wife and Child?

ROGER
In the Chamber with the Milch-Nurse.

GET-ALL
My Family is well increased since I have been a Platonick Husband and Father.

ROGER
I hope your Worship will not want Heirs to inherit your Wealth?

GET-ALL
No, no, I cannot want Heirs, the way being so easie to get them.

ROGER
But hath not your Worship a mind to get her with Child, after a Corporeal manner?

GET-ALL
Faith Roger, she is tempting, being young and handsome; but if I should get her with Child as our fore-fathers got us, I fear this Learned age will punish me, either with death or intolerable Fines.

ROGER
But if there be no Witness, they cannot prove it; for this Platonick Son and Heir of your Worships, appears as if it had been got by a Corporeal action.

GET-ALL
You say true; wherefore call your Mistress.

[The while he Walks, Enter **MISTRESS PEG**.

GET-ALL
My Imaginary Wife, how doth our Imaginary Son?

PEG
Very well, Sir.

GET-ALL
But doth he Corporeally suck?

PEG
Yes Sir.

GET-ALL
I wonder at that; but my greatest wonder is, how that an Incorporeal Conception, should come to be a Corporeal Child!

PEG
'Tis like Spirits that take Bodies, Sir.

GET-ALL
But may I not lawfully get you with Child after a Corporeal manner?

PEG
Yes surely, Sir.

GET-ALL
Then let us go to bed, and try if I can get a Child after the old Corporeal way, for I never knew when this Child was gotten.

PEG

But I must be Ceremoniously Married first.

GET-ALL

Hang Ceremony, those Children never come to good that are got with Ceremony.

PEG

But I cannot lie with you Corporeally, unless you honestly marry me.

GET-ALL

But I tell you, I did not know when I got this Child which I am forced to own.

PEG

'Tis true, Sir; but that was begot by your Idea, and my Imagination, and not personally; wherefore, if you desire to lie with me, you must first Marry me, otherwise the Law will severely punish us, and they would be glad we should give them that occasion, that they might take away your Wealth.

GET-ALL

Faith, thou shall rather breed by Conceit, then I Marry really; but if we must not lie together Corporeally, may not we kiss Corporeally?

PEG

Truly Sir, I did never kiss any Man but in the way of a civil Salute.

GET-ALL

But did not my Idea and your Imagination kiss?

PEG

Yes Sir, but not Corporeally.

GET-ALL

Faith, I have a Natural desire to thee; but I dare not Marry thee, for fear I should be made a Cuckold, as I have been made a Father.

PEG

Truly I am very Chast, and shall make a very honest Wife; and if you will promise to Marry me, I will discover by whom you have been deceived.

GET-ALL

If you can prove your self honest, I will.

PEG

Then know Sir, This Child which is laid to your Charge, is none of mine, but a Bastard of my Brother's, Captain Valour; but by reason my Brother was ruin'd in the Civil Wars, and I having lost my Portion in his ruine, I had not Means to maintain me honestly, according to my quality; wherefore, hearing you were a very worthy person, and Rich, and an unmarried Man, I desired my Brother's assistance in the design of getting you to be my Husband; but the design could not take effect if we had not counterfeited a

Spiritual Court and Judge, which Judge was Mr. Traveller; and the Doctor Mr. Will Fullwit; and the Lawyer was Mr. Sencible; and my Brothers, Lieutenant and Major, Witnesses; all gallant valiant Men, but poor Cavaliers; so that the design was honest, but the management was full of deceit.

GET-ALL
But what was she that was the Midwife.

PEG
An honest ancient Gentlewoman, whose Husband was kill'd in the Wars.

GET-ALL
Well, since you have so ingenuously told me the truth, I will Marry thee for thy honest wit; for he's a fool that will marry a fool.

[Enter **JUDGES** as in a Court of Judicature, and **SERJEANT BARRISTER** as a Pleader at the Bar, and his **CLERK** with a bag of Papers; also **HARRY SENCIBLE** as the Defendant, and **WILL FULLWIT** and **DICK TRAVELLER** as Witnesses, the **CAPTAIN** as a Plaintiff, and the **LIEUTENANT** and **ANCIENT** as Witnesses.

SERJEANT
May it please your Lordships, I am here to Plead in my Clients behalf against Mr. Sencible, who against the Laws of Honour, Honesty, and Civil Government, hath a young Gentlewoman of good Birth and Education (but poor) in his keeping, not by the Gentlewoman's (or Friends) Consent, but by constraint and force, inclosing her in a Chamber, under Locks and Bolts, lest she should escape from him.

JUDGE
Where is your Witnesses?

LIEUTENANT
Here my Lords.

JUDGE
Will you both Swear these Accusations for a truth?

LIEUTENANT
We are ready to Swear whensoever the Book is offered.

JUDGE
What says the Defendant?

HARRY
My Lords, I will confess the truth, but I desire Justice, and that my Accusation against Serjeant Plead-all, may be heard.

SERJEANT
Good my Lords, grant his Request; for I fear not what can be said against me.

JUDGE
We grant his Request.

HARRY

Then my Lords, I freely confess that I have such a Gentlewoman in my keeping, as I am accused, and do keep her under Lock and Key; not for fear she should leave me, but for fear some man should steal her away from me; for in this age Men are like hungry Wolves, seeking to devour the Virginity and Reputation of young handsome Women: But this young Gentlewoman who I do so carefully keep, is my own Natural Sister, which these two worthy Gentlemen, Mr. Fullwit and Mr. Traveller, will witness; besides, I can bring all my Neighbours that will witness the same; and since Serjeant Plead-all hath endeavoured to disgrace me, not only before your Lordships, but before a Court full of People; I think it not unmeet, for me to declare to your Lordships, That Serjeant Plead-all hath at this present kept in his House a Gentlewoman, as a Servant, in Man's Clothes, whose Birth and Breeding is better then his own.

SERJEANT

My Lords, I deny his Impeachment; and if he can prove that I have a Woman in Man's Clothes, that is a Houshold Servant of mine, I will Marry her, were she an old Witch.

HARRY

My Lords, this Assembly is sufficient witness of what he hath said, as also what I have said; and to prove what I say is true, here is the Gentlewoman who serves him as his Clerk, in Man's Clothes, she is Sister to Mr. Fullwit, which he and others will witness, and she her self confesses.

JANE

My Lords, I do confess I am a Woman, and out of love to Serjeant Plead-all did take this disguise, which I hope is pardonable, since it is not a breach of the Laws of the Kingdom, whatsoever it may be in modesty.

SERJEANT

How is this! my Clerk a Woman! and must be my Wife! I am finely cozen'd i'faith!

HARRY

We beseech your Lordships to give your Judgment.

JUDGES

Our Judgment is,
That you are free, and the Serjeant must Marry his She-Clerk.

[Exeunt.

SCENE II

[Enter **FATHER**, with his **DAUGHTER**.

DAUGHTER

Pray Sir, tell me whether you approve of my Choice?

FATHER

To speak truly, Daughter, you have chosen very wisely; but how your Youth will agree with Age, I cannot tell.

DAUGHTER
Never fear it Sir, for I shall love Age in a Husband, better then Youth in my self.

FATHER
Well, Heaven bless you.

[Enter a **MESSENGER** from the young Suiters.

MESSENGER
Sir, Report says, that the Lady your Daughter, is to be Married to an ancient Man, to the great disgrace of her other Suiters, Youth, Beauty, and Bravery; and therefore they desire, that before she Marries, she would be pleased to give them all a publick Audience.

FATHER
Daughter, answer this Gentleman.

DAUGHTER
Sir, pray tell them, that I cannot civilly deny their Request, in case they'l be pleased to give me leave to make a publick answer.

MESSENGER
No question, Madam, but they will, and I shall inform them of what you say.

[Exeunt.

ACT V

SCENE I

[Enter **MRS JANE FULLWIT** in her Woman's Habit, and **SERJEANT PLEAD-ALL**.

SERJEANT
WELL Mistress, your Wit and your Person hath not only excused your deceit, but I am so in Love with you, that I would not but have been deceived for all the World.

JANE
Sir, with your pardon, there is one more deceived besides your self, and another like to be.

SERJEANT
Who be those?

JANE
He that is deceived, is Get-all the Usurer, and he that shall be deceived is Doctor Cure-all.

SERJEANT
What, my two Rivals?

JANE
Yes Sir.

SERJEANT
Then they cannot laugh at me.

JANE
If they do, you may laugh at them again.

SERJEANT
I would the old Lady was deceived.

JANE
She will in a short time.

SERJEANT
Faith, I find that the Cavaliers are the best deceivers.

JANE
They have been so oft deceived themselves, that they have learned by their misfortunes.

SERJEANT
But we will not deceive each other, but go to your Brother to dispatch our Marriage.

[Exeunt.

[Enter **CAPTAIN**, **LIEUTENANT**, **CORNET**, and **WILL FULLWIT**, then enters **HARRY** in a Chamber-Maid's Habit.

WILL
Mrs. Harry you are welcome, how doth your good Lady?

[She makes a Curtsie ill-favouredly.

HARRY
My Lady at this time is troubled with Love in the Heart, and Gout in the Toe.

CAPTAIN
Is Dick Traveller the cause of the Love-sick heart?

HARRY
No, it is the Lawyer's young Clerk.

WILL

He is discovered.

HARRY
Yes, but I will not suffer any to inform her of it.

CORNET
But if her mind be so young, I doubt we may despair of our design.

[Enter **DICK TRAVELLER**.

DICK
Mrs. Harry, give me leave to salute you.

[He makes a Curtsie, and he salutes him.

DICK
Faith Harry, you kiss like a Woman; I pray Jove you be not turn'd Female with wearing a Petticoat.

HARRY
If I be, I pray Jove I may not be such a Female as my old Lady is.

DICK
But how goeth on our design?

HARRY
Fast towards a young man, but slowly towards a gray head.

DICK
What young Man?

HARRY
The Lawyer's Clerk.

DICK
What is she in Love with honest Jack? but she is discovered.

HARRY
But she knows not of it, for she is almost desperate; and between every groan of pain, she sighs for Love.

DICK
Why, then there is no hopes for me.

HARRY
Not unless you are presented in the Name of the Clerk, and marryed by Candle-light; for she being half blind, will never distinguish which is which.

CAPTAIN

Faith, Harry 's Counsel is good.

WILL
But if she be as deaf as she is blind, we shall not need to dissemble his Name.

DICK
But Harry, do you think she will live long?

HARRY
My only fear is, she will hardly live so long that he may be Married to her.

DICK
I hope she is not so desperately sick.

LIEUTENANT
If she should die before Dick is marryed, we are all undone.

CORNET
If she should, it would be worse then our Cashiering.

WILL
Take comfort Gentlemen, for old Women are such dry and tough meat, that Death cannot set his Teeth into them, nor his Dart enter them.

CAPTAIN
Will says true; for perchance she may last longer then Dick would have her.

DICK
I would have her live till I am marryed to her, and then let her die assoon as she will.

HARRY
Well Gentlemen, I dare stay no longer for fear my Lady should chide me most grievously.

WILL
Thou art a most grievous Rogue.

[Exit **HARRY**.

[Enter **SERJEANT** and **JANE**.

WILL
Hey-day, who comes here!

SERJEANT
We are come to have you for a Witness to our Marriage, since you proved so good a one at the Bar.

WILL
Stay so long, till we see an end of our Comedy.

SERJEANT
If your Comedy be long, I shall not have patience.

CAPTAIN
It shall be short, and you shall have more Bridals to accompany you.

[Enter **HARRY**.

HARRY
I have been at home with my Mistress; but all the plot of Jack Clerk was revealed to her, whilst I was here; O Mr. Plead-all, I cry you mercy, I saw you not.

SERJEANT
Nay, Mrs. Harry pray conceal not any thing for my being here; for I thank you, I am now become one of the Society.

HARRY
And how do you like of the Acquaintance.

SERJEANT
So well, as I would not be a stranger for any other good.

HARRY
I presume Mrs. Jane hath pleased you well.

SERJEANT
So well, as I am confident I shall be happy in my Marriage: But how doth the old Lady take the discovery of my She-Clerk?

HARRY
Faith, as ill as she would take the discovery of her He-Chamber-Maid; the truth is, she hath been in such passions, as she is almost transform'd to Mummy.

SERJEANT
That she was before the discovery.

HARRY
But now she is more perfect Mummy then she was; but I, to comfort her, have promised to bring her a handsome young Man, only he is taller and bigger, as being a Man; and I did reason with her so long, that I have perswaded her to love a Man, rather then a Boy.

CAPTAIN
And will she come to reason?

HARRY
She will, upon condition he be a young Man.

DICK

But how shall I make my self appear to be a young Man?

CAPTAIN

You are not so old, but you may appear in the dark to be a young Man.

CAPTAIN

Appear, say you! how the Devil can he appear in the dark?

HARRY

Well, for the good of the Common-Weale, I have devised a way, how Dick shall appear like a young Man to a blind eye.

WILL

Faith, I know no difference between the dark and a blind eye.

HARRY

Hang you, a Pox of you all, I meant a dim eye.

DICK

Come, dim or blind, let's hear your design.

HARRY

This is the design, Dick shall first shave as close as may be, and then paint his Face, and with a handsome Perriwig, and fine Clothes, he will appear a Young Man to an Old Woman.

WILL

Faith, the Paint must be laid on his Face as thick as Morter on a Wall, otherwise his age will be seen.

CAPTAIN

Not to a dim eye.

DICK

Why, I have not such Wrincles in my face as requires much filling up.

HARRY

I will warrant you, that I will get such an Artist, that if Dick 's Wrincles were as deep as a Sawpit, they should be clos'd up, and his face appear fair and even, if not smooth; wherefore Dick, get a handsome Perriwig, and put on your best Suit of Clothes, and I will send a Painter to your Chamber; then go to her, for she expects thee, and carry a Priest, and some Witnesses, and Marry her.

WILL

Will not you be there?

HARRY

I cannot, but I have left those in her house that shall conduct you to her; but I must go about my Sisters affairs, where I must desire all the Company to meet me at Doctor Cure-all 's House.

ALL SPEAK
We will not fail you.

DICK
But the Cornet and Lieutenant must go with me to be my Witnesses.

HARRY
Take them!

[Exeunt.

[Enter **DOCTOR CURE-ALL** and his **MAN**.

DOCTOR CURE-ALL
Give me my Cloak, for now the Clerk being proved a Woman, I hope the old Lady will accept of me, and that will be a double good fortune; first, that my Rival is cheated; next, that I shall be Master of the Ladies Riches.

MAN
Doth your Worship mean the old Lady?

DOCTOR
Who should I mean else?

MAN
Sir, she was Married last Night, about one of the Clock, as her Servant told me this Morning.

DOCTOR
Married! to whom?

MAN
To a young Cavalier, one Mr. Dick Traveller.

DOCTOR
What the Devil, hath he Married her?

MAN
I know not whether the Devil Married them, but certainly they are Married.

DOCTOR
Why, he is older then I.

MAN
He hath past for a young Man with the Lady.

[Enter another **MAN**.

2ND MAN
Sir, there's a young Gentlewoman desires to speak with your Worship.

DOCTOR
'Tis some comfort to converse with a young Woman, after the loss of an old—

[The **DOCTOR** goes forth, and enters leading **MRS ANNE SENCIBLE**.

DOCTOR
Lady, wherein may I serve you?

ANNE
Sir, I am to desire your assistance for the Cure of a Disease I am troubled with.

DOCTOR
What Disease?

ANNE
The Disease is Love.

DOCTOR
Truly, Lady, a Physician hath no Remedy for that Disease, unless the Party be in Love with the Physician.

ANNE
The truth is, Sir, I am in Love with you.

DOCTOR
With me Lady!

[Enter **HARRY SENCIBLE**, and when he enters, he sees his Sister, he starts back and frowns, she seems to be afraid.

HARRY
Is the Doctor and you so well acquainted, as you two to be private alone.

ANNE
Truly I was never here before.

HARRY
'Tis false.

DOCTOR
I will assure you, Mr. Sencible, she speaks truth, for she was never here to my knowledg before.

HARRY

I perceive you both agree in a Story, and I take it as an affront you should entertain my Sister in private.

DOCTOR
I vow to Heaven I never saw her before this time, nor knew I that you were her Brother.

HARRY
This answer will not serve me, for I will have satisfaction; and as for you, Sister, I will offer you up as a Sacrifice to Honour.

[He draws his Sword, she shreeks out, and runs behind the **DOCTOR**, the **DOCTOR** strives to defend her.

DOCTOR
Sir, 'Tis unworthy to draw you Sword upon a Woman, or to fight with an unarmed Man.

HARRY
I do not intend to fight with you at this time, but to kill my Sister.

DOCTOR
For what?

HARRY
For visiting a Man, and being alone with him in his Chamber.

DOCTOR
Why is that such a Crime?

HARRY
'Tis such a Crime, that unless she can prove she is Married, or assured, I will kill her.

ANNE
Good Doctor save my life.

DOCTOR
Then Sir, give me leave to tell you, we are agreed to Marry, may we have your consent?

HARRY
I must have time to ask the advice of some dear Friends first.

ANNE
Dear Brother consent, without advice.

HARRY
That I will not.

ANNE
Then send for your Friends hither.

HARRY

I have no body here to send.

DOCTOR
You may have two or three of my Servants if you please.

[Enter a **MAN**.

MAN
There is two Gentlemen below that desire to speak with Mr. Sencible.

HARRY
They are come as I desired, pray bring them in.

[Enter **WILL FULLWIT**, and the **CAPTAIN**.

Dear Will, and Captain, I was sending for you both, to ask your advice about a Cause that hath much troubled me, which is a great concernment both to my Justice and Honour.

WILL
What is that?

HARRY
I coming to see Doctor Cure-all, found my Sister out of my House, discoursing here alone with the Doctor, which is a great discredit for a young Virgin, to be not only abroad without attendance, but in Company with a Man alone, and in his Chamber.

CAPTAIN
That is not well, I did not believe Mrs. Anne Sencible would have done such an act.

DOCTOR
Gentlemen, the Lady is in no fault, for she and I are agreed to marry, if her Brother consents.

WILL
That is another Case; and will not you give your consent Harry?

HARRY
I cannot tell.

CAPTAIN
Come, come, you shall consent.

WILL
Yes, yes, you shall Harry; Doctor give me your hand, and Mrs. Sencible give me yours, so joyn them together; do you agree truly and really to Marry?

BOTH ANSWER
We do.

CAPTAIN
Then, Mr. Sencible, give them joy of their Contract.

HARRY
I wish you Both joy.

[Enter to the **DOCTOR**, **MRS PEG VALOROSA**, **GET-ALL**, **SERJEANT PLEAD-ALL**, and **MRS JANE FULLWIT**.

GET-ALL
Come, come, Captain Valorous, let us go to the Church, for I am impatient.

SERJEANT
Not so impatient as I.

CAPTAIN
Faith, we come in here but to take another Couple along with us.

GET-ALL
Are they agreed?

HARRY
They are, they are; there only wants that Ceremony,
You do, and all is sure.

[Enter **DICK TRAVELLER**, **LIEUTENANT** and **CORNET**.

DICK
I am come only to make one to fill up the Matrimonial Triumphs.

HARRY
How doth my old Lady like the young Blade?

DICK
So well, as she is so well pleased, as it hath made her half young again.

[Enter **MISTRESS INFORMER**.

DICK
Welcome Mrs. Informer.

INFORMER
By my troth, my heart did tremble, for fear I should not come time enough to these fortunate Nuptials.

GET-ALL
Well, to let all this Company see, that I the first deceived, am as well, if not better, pleased then the deceivers; here I do promise to give my Brother, that must be Captain Valorous, Twenty thousand pounds to maintain his Bastards, to discharge his Whores, and to Marry a Virtuous and Honourable Wife; also, I give Doctor Feel-pulse, Will Fullwit, Five thousand pounds; and Harry Sencible Five thousand

more; and Five thousand pound to the Lieutenant; and Five thousand pounds between the Cornet and Mrs. Informer; as for my Judg Dick Traveller, I did intend to have fee'd him well, and to give him money to have bought a place in the Arches, but he is better provided.

SERJEANT
I cannot present the whole Society, but I will make my Brother Fullwit's Five thousand pounds, you gave him, Ten.

DOCTOR
So will I give as much to my Brother Harry Sencible.

DICK
And I will present the rest of the Society.

WILL
Let's go unto Church to make all sure,
For nothing in Extreams will long endure.

CAPTAIN
Stay we must go to the Hearing of my Cousin
Prudence 's Cause first, and then we shall have another couple.

SCENE III

[The Scene is a Publick Hall, or Pleading-Court, wherein is a Publick Assembly, the **YOUNG SUITERS** and some other **GALLANTS**, taking one Bar, and the **YOUNG LADY** and her **OLD SUITER** another; and all **BRIDAL COUPLES**.

[One of the **YOUNG SUITERS** speaks.

YOUNG SUITER
Most Noble Auditors.
I am chosen by my fellow-Sufferers to declare the Injustice and Injury this young Lady has done us, and her self, by refusing us that are young, handsome, healthy and strong, for an old, infirm, weak and decayed Man, who has neither a clear Eye-sight to admire her Beauty, nor a perfect Hearing to be informed of her Wit; nor sufficient Strength to fight in her behalf, or defend her Honour; nor that heat of affection that he can love her as she deserves. Indeed, it is not to be suffer'd that Old Men and Women should Marry Young Persons; for it is as much as to tie or bind the Living and Dead together; for, though it cannot be truly said, that old age is dead, yet we may say, 'tis rotten, and Corruption is next to death; for all Creatures corrupt before they dissolve; and we are taught by our holy Fathers, that we must put off the Old Man, and put on the New Man: Wherefore, 'tis not lawful for this young Lady to Marry that old Man, it being both against Church and State, as not profitable to either, but disadvantagious to both.

THE LADIES ANSWER
Most Noble Auditors,

I come not here to express either my Wit or Malice, but to defend my honest Cause, and to express my true Love; Wherefore, I shall briefly answer this Gentleman's Objections: First, as for the Injustice he accuses me of, I utterly deny that I am guilty, for to make a lawful Choice is no Injustice to them; and to refuse a young Man before an old and wise one, is no Injury to my self; Next, what he says of their Handsomness, Health and Strength; I answer, that in my opinion, a handsome Man is an error in Nature, and Health and Strength are very uncertain in young Men, for their Vices decay one, and impair the other, before their Natural time; whereas, the Infirmities of Old Age are Natural, neither infectious, unwholsome or dangerous to their Wives: And though ancient Men have not their Hearing so quick, nor their Eye-sight so clear as young Men, yet have they quicker Wits, and clearer Understandings, acquired by long Experience of all sorts of Actions, Humors, Customs, Discourses, Accidents, and Fortuns amongst Mankind; Wherefore, old Men cannot chuse but be more Knowing, Rational and Wise then Young. Concerning the Church and State, since they do allow of buying and selling young Maids to Men to be their Wives, they cannot condemn those Maids that make their bargain to their own advantage, and chuse rather to be bought then sold, and I confess I am one of the number of those; for I'le rather chuse an old Man that buys me with his Wealth, then a young one, whom I must purchase with my Wealth; who, after he has wasted my Estate, may sell me to Misery and Poverty. Wherefore, our Sex may well pray, From Young Mens ignorance and follies, from their pride, vanity and prodigality, their gaming, quarelling, drinking and whoring, their pocky and diseased bodies, their Mortgages, Debts and Serjeants, their Whores and Bastards, and from all such sorts of Vices and Miseries that are frequent amongst Young Men, Good Lord deliver Us. But for fear of such a Misfortune as to be a Wife to a young Man, I will Marry this ancient Man, and so, Cousins, I am, if you please, ready to wait on you to Church.

MARGARET CAVENDISH – A CONCISE BIBLIOGRAPHY

Philosophical Fancies (1653)
Poems and Fancies (1653)
Philosophical and Physical Opinions (1655)
Nature's Pictures drawn by Fancie's Pencil to the Life (1656)
The World's Olio (1655)
Playes, (1662) folio, containing twenty-one plays including
Loves Adventures
The Several Wits
Youths Glory, and Deaths Banquet
The Lady Contemplation
Wits Cabal
The Unnatural Tragedy
The Public Wooing
The Matrimonial Trouble
Nature's Three Daughters (Beauty, Love and Wit) Part I & Part II
The Religious
The Comical Hash
Bell in Campo
A Comedy of the Apocryphal Ladies
The Female Academy
Plays never before printed (1668), containing five plays.
The Sociable Companions, or the Female Wits

The Presence
The Bridals
The Convent of Pleasure
A Piece of a Play
Orations of Divers Sorts (1662)
Philosophical Letters, or Modest Reflections upon some Opinions in Natural Philosophy maintained by several learned authors of the age (1664)
CCXI Sociable Letters (1664)
Observations upon Experimental Philosophy & Description of a New World (1666)
The Blazing World (1666)
The Life of William Cavendish, Duke, Marquis, and Earl of Newcastle, Earl of Ogle, Viscount Mansfield, and Baron of Bolsover, of Ogle, Bothal, and Hepple, &c. (1667)
Grounds of Natural Philosophy (1668)

www.ingramcontent.com/pod-product-compliance
Lightning Source LLC
Chambersburg PA
CBHW021935170626
46807CB00007B/3115